William Shakespeare's The Two Noble Kinsmen: A Retelling in Prose

David Bruce

Published by David Bruce, 2022.

This is a work of fiction. Similarities to real people, places, or events are entirely coincidental.

WILLIAM SHAKESPEARE'S THE TWO NOBLE KINSMEN: A RETELLING IN PROSE

First edition. July 29, 2022.

ISBN: 979-8201069278

Written by David Bruce.

Table of Contents

Cover Image for William Shakespeare's *The Two Noble Kinsmen*: A Retelling in Prose:

A Tourney, c1470.

Chroniques d'Angleterre.

BnF MS. fr. 87, fol. 58v.

Educate Yourself
Read Like A Wolf Eats
Be Excellent to Each Other
Books Then, Books Now, Books Forever

***

In this retelling, as in all my retellings, I have tried to make the work of literature accessible to modern readers who may lack the knowledge about mythology, religion, and history that the literary work's contemporary audience had.

Do you know a language other than English? If you do, I give you permission to translate this book, copyright your translation, publish or self-publish it, and keep all the royalties for yourself. (Do give me credit, of course, for the original retelling.)

I would like to see my retellings of classic literature used in schools, so I give permission to the country of Finland (and all other countries) to give copies of this book to all students forever. I also give permission to the state of Texas (and all other states) to give copies of this book to all students forever. I also give permission to all teachers to give copies of this book to all students forever.

Teachers need not actually teach my retellings. Teachers are welcome to give students copies of my eBooks as background material. For example, if they are teaching Homer's *Iliad* and *Odyssey*, teachers are welcome to give students copies of my *Virgil's* Aeneid: *A Retelling in Prose* and tell students, "Here's another ancient epic you may want to read in your spare time."

Dedicated to Jimmy Durante and Eddie Cantor

Comedians Jimmy Durante and Eddie Cantor were very giving of their time to good causes. On New Year's Day of 1943, Mr. Durante met Mr. Cantor while taking a walk. "Eddie," Mr. Durante said, "I'm just thinkin'. This must be a tough time for the guys over there in that hospital. Here it's New Year's Day, they're sick, some of 'em have amputations. What do ya say we go over and entertain?" The two comedians rehearsed for a short time, then entertained at the hospital from 10:30 a.m. to 5 p.m. Afterward, Mr. Durante said hoarsely to Mr. Cantor, "Eddie, tell me, don't a t'ing like dis make ya feel good?"

CAST OF CHARACTERS

ARCITE and PALAMON, *the two noble kinsmen, first cousins, nephews of Creon, King of Thebes.*

THESEUS, Duke of Athens.

HIPPOLYTA, Queen of the Amazons, later Duchess of Athens.

EMILIA, her sister. She is sometimes called Emily.

PIRITHOUS, friend to Theseus.

Three QUEENS, widows of the Kings killed while laying siege to Thebes.

The JAILER of Theseus' prison.

The Jailer's DAUGHTER.

The Jailer's BROTHER.

The WOOER of the Jailer's daughter.

Two FRIENDS of the Jailer.

A DOCTOR.

ARTESIUS, an Athenian soldier.

VALERIUS, a Theban.

WOMAN, attending on Emilia.

An Athenian GENTLEMAN.

Six KNIGHTS, three accompanying Arcite, and three accompanying Palamon.

Six COUNTRYMEN, one dressed as a BAVIAN or baboon.

A SCHOOLMASTER. His name is Gerald.

NELL, a countrywoman.

A TABORER.

A singing BOY, a HERALD, MESSENGERS, a SERVANT.

Hymen (god of weddings), lords, soldiers, four countrywomen (Fritz, Maudlin, Luce, and Barbary), nymphs, attendants, maids, executioner, guard.

Nota Bene

John Fletcher is thought to be the co-author of this play.

PROLOGUE

The Prologue says this to you the audience:

"New plays and maidenheads are much alike. Both are much sought after, and for both much money is given, if they stand sound and well. And a good play, whose modest scenes blush on its marriage day and shiver to lose its virginity, is like a wife who after a holy wedding and the first night's sexual activity is still the image of modesty, and retains still more of the virgin maiden, according to one's sight, than a woman who has been subject to her husband's sexual pains and pangs.

"We pray our work of art may be so, for I am sure it has a noble and pure father: A learned and more famous poet never yet has walked between the Po River in Italy and the silver Trent River in England. Geoffrey Chaucer, who is admired by all, gives us the story we will recount. 'The Knight's Tale' lives in his *Canterbury Tales* and is there fixed in eternity.

"If we fail to live up to the nobleness of Chaucer's story, and the first sound this child — our work of art — hears is a hiss from you the audience, how it will shake the bones of that good man Chaucer and make him cry from underground, 'Oh, fan from me the witless chaff of such a writer who blasts my laurel wreath and makes my famed works lighter and of less worth than the folktales of Robin Hood!'"

This society used winnowing fans to blow away the worthless chaff or husks from the valuable grain. This society also regarded tales of folklore as being of less value than courtly literary romances.

The Prologue continued, "This is the fear we bring. For, to say the truth, it would be a never-ending, impossible, and too ambitious thing to aspire to match Chaucer, weak as we are. We, almost breathless, are unable to swim in the deep water of his literary worth.

"If you only hold out your helping hands and applaud us, we shall turn about in the wind of your applause and do something to save ourselves. You shall hear scenes that, although they are below Chaucer's art, may yet be worth two hours' travel and travail. We will work to take you on an imaginative journey.

"We wish sweet sleep to Chaucer's bones; we wish happiness to you. If this work of art does not keep dullness away from you for a short time, we perceive that our losses fall so thickly that we must necessarily stop appearing in works of art."

CHAPTER 1

— 1.1 —

Music played as a wedding procession arrived.

Singing and strewing flowers, a boy in a white robe arrived.

Holding a burning torch, Hymen, the god of marriage, arrived.

Bearing a wheaten garland, a nymph with her tresses unbound arrived. Garlands made of wheat stalks are a traditional symbol of fertility.

Between two other nymphs who were wearing wheaten garlands on their heads, Theseus, the Duke of Athens, arrived.

Hippolyta, Theseus' bride, arrived; her hair was loose and hanging down. Theseus' friend Pirithous led her, and another man held a garland over her head. Loose hair is a traditional symbol of virginity.

Emilia, who was holding up the train of Hippolyta's dress, arrived. Emilia was Hippolyta's sister.

Finally Artesius, who was an Athenian soldier, and some attendants arrived.

This is the song the boy sang:

"Roses, their sharp spines [thorns] being gone,

"Not royal in their smells alone,

"But also in their hue;

"Maiden pinks, of odor faint,

"Daisies smell-less, yet most quaint [pretty],

"And sweet thyme true;

"Primrose, firstborn child of Ver [Spring],

"Merry springtime's harbinger,

"With her bells [its flowers] dim;

"Oxlips in their cradles growing,"

The leaves of the oxlip form a kind of cradle as they grow around the flower's bud.

"Marigolds on deathbeds [graves] blowing [blossoming],

"Lark's-heels [Larkspur] trim."

The boy strew flowers as he sang:

"All dear Nature's children sweet
"Lie before bride and bridegroom's feet,
"Blessing their sense.
"Not an angel [good bird] of the air,
"Bird melodious or bird fair [beautiful],
"Is absent hence.
"The crow, the sland'rous cuckoo, nor"

The cuckoo is slanderous because its cry mocks married men by calling them cuckolds.

"The boding [ominous] raven, nor chough hoar [gray-headed jackdaw],
"Nor chatt'ring pie [magpie],
"May on our bridehouse [house that is a wedding site] perch or sing,
"Or with them any discord bring,
"But from it fly."

Three Queens arrived, dressed all in black, with black veils stained with tears and travel, and wearing imperial crowns. The First Queen fell down at the foot of Theseus; the Second Queen fell down at the foot of Hippolyta; the Third Queen fell down at the foot of Emilia.

The First Queen said to Theseus, "For pity's sake and the sake of true gentility, hear and respect me. Pay attention to what I have to say."

The Second Queen said to Hippolyta, "For your mother's sake, and as you wish your womb may thrive with fair ones, hear and respect me."

The Third Queen said to Emilia, "Now for the love of your future husband — him whom Jove, King of the gods, has destined to be your distinguished bridegroom and the honor of your bed — and for the sake of pure and unsullied virginity, be the advocate for us and our distresses. This good deed shall erase all your evil deeds that are now set down in the Book of Trespasses kept in Heaven."

Theseus said to the First Queen, "Sad lady, rise."

Hippolyta said to the Second Queen, "Stand up."

Emilia said to the Third Queen, "Bend no knees to me. Whatever distressed woman whom I may help binds me to her — I will help her."

Theseus said to the First Queen, "What's your request? Speak for all of you Queens."

The First Queen replied, "We are three Queens whose sovereigns fell before the wrath of cruel Creon; our husbands have endured the beaks of ravens, talons of kites, and pecks of crows in the foul fields of Thebes."

The husbands of the three Queens had taken part in the war of the Seven Against Thebes and had been killed. After King Oedipus of Thebes had died, his two sons, Eteocles and Polynices, quarreled over who should rule Thebes. Polynices gathered other Kings as allies and attacked Thebes. Both Eteocles and Polynices died in the battle, and Creon, their uncle, became the ruler of Thebes. Creon forbid the corpses of those who had attacked Thebes to be buried; those unburied corpses were now being eaten by birds and reduced to skeletons.

The First Queen continued, "Creon will not allow us to burn their bones, to put their ashes in urns, nor to take the offense of mortal loathsomeness from the blessed eye of holy Phoebus, but instead Creon allows the corpses to infect the winds with the stench of our slain lords."

Phoebus Apollo is the god who drives the Sun-chariot across the sky each day.

Wives in this culture referred to their husbands as lords.

The First Queen continued, "Oh, have pity, Theseus, Duke of Athens! You have purged the Earth of robbers and monsters. You purger of the Earth, draw your feared sword that does good turns to the world; give us the bones of our dead Kings so that we may place them in a chapel. And of your boundless goodness take some note that for our crowned heads we have no roof except this sky above us, which is the lion's and the bear's roof and the vault above everything."

"Please, don't kneel," Theseus replied. "Because I was transported with your speech, I allowed your knees to wrong themselves. I have heard about the fortunes of your dead lords, which gives me such lamenting that it awakens my vengeance and revenge for them.

"King Capaneus was your lord and husband. The day that he was to marry you, at such an occasion as now is with me, I met your groom by that altar of Mars. You were at that time beautiful — Juno's mantle was not more beautiful than your hair, nor did her mantle more luxuriantly envelope her than your hair that was bountifully spread around you. Your wheaten wreath was then neither threshed nor blasted. You were still an unreaped virgin and the future death of your husband had not then blighted you. Lady Fortune looked at you and dimpled her cheek with smiles. Hercules, my kinsman, looked at you and, being made weak by the beauty of your eyes, laid down his club. He tumbled down upon the hide of the lion of Nemea that he had slain and swore that his muscles grew soft."

Another time that Heracles' muscles grew soft was when he served Queen Omphale of Lydia as a slave for a year and was forced to do women's work and wear women's clothing. Eventually, Queen Omphale freed Hercules and married him.

Theseus continued, "Oh, grief and time, those two fearful consumers, devour everything!"

He was shocked by the transformation of the First Queen from virgin bride to mourning widow.

The First Queen said, "Oh, I hope that some god has put his mercy in your manliness, to which he'll infuse power, and press you to go forth and undertake to help us bury the corpses of our husbands."

Theseus said, "Oh, bend no knees to me, bend none, widow! Bend your knees to the helmeted Bellona, Roman goddess of war, and pray for me, who will be your soldier. I am troubled."

The First Queen rose, and Theseus turned away. He would be her soldier, but he knew that this would be a formidable undertaking; he would have to make war against Creon and Thebes.

The Second Queen addressed Hippolyta, who had been Queen of the warrior women known as the Amazons. Hippolyta and Theseus had fought each other with their armies. Theseus narrowly won the battle and had fallen in love with Hippolyta; today was their wedding day.

The Second Queen said, "Honored Hippolyta, most dreaded Amazonian, who has slain the scythe-tusked boar; who with your arm, as strong as it is white, was close to making men captive to your sex, except that this Theseus, your lord, who was born to uphold creation in that honor nature first styled it in, shrunk you into the bounds that you were overflowing, at once subduing your force and your affection."

This society believed that men were by nature superior to women. Hippolyta had come close to defeating Theseus and his army, but Theseus had been born to uphold the superiority of men and so had eventually defeated

Hippolyta and her women warriors. He had defeated Hippolyta and caused her to fall in love with him.

The Second Queen continued, "You, Hippolyta, are a soldieress who equally balances sternness with pity, whom now I know have much more power over him — Theseus — than he ever had on you, who own his strength and his love, too. Theseus is a servant who obeys even the implications of any speech made by you, dear model of ladies. Tell him to help us, whom flaming war scorches, so that we may cool ourselves under the shadow of his sword. Ask him to lift his sword over our heads. Speak your request in a woman's voice, like such a woman as any of us three; weep rather than fail. Lend us a knee; kneel down with us but touch the ground for us no longer time than a dove moves when its head is plucked off. Tell him what you would do if he lay swollen on the blood-soaked battlefield, showing the Sun his teeth and grinning at the Moon."

Hippolyta replied, "Poor lady, say no more. I would rather pursue this good action with you as that to which I am going — my wedding — and yet I have never so willingly gone this way.

"Theseus, my lord, has been affected to the depth of his heart with your distress; let him think for a moment. I'll speak to him very soon."

The Second Queen rose.

The Third Queen said, "Oh, I set down my petition coldly, as if I were writing on ice, but my hot grief thawed and melted it into drops of water; in the same way, sorrow, lacking other forms of expression, is pressed out in the form of tears by deeply felt grief. Grief cannot be adequately expressed in a cold petition; it must be felt and expressed in hot tears."

Emilia said, "Please stand up. Your grief is written on your cheek."

"Oh, grief!" the Third Queen said. "You cannot read it there on my cheek."

The Third Queen rose.

She pointed to her eyes and said, "There through my tears, like pebbles that seemed wrinkled and distorted when looked at in a glassy, mirrory stream, you may behold my sorrows. Lady, lady, it's a pity! He who will know all the treasure of the Earth must dig to the center, too; he who will fish for my smallest minnow, let him put a lead weight on his line to sink it and catch one at my heart. Anyone who wants to know the depth of my sorrow must look into my heart."

Realizing that what she had said could be interpreted as implying that Emilia lacked perceptiveness, the Third Queen apologized: "Oh, pardon me! Extreme suffering, that sharpens some minds, makes me a fool who speaks extravagantly."

"Please say nothing," Emilia said. "Please. A person who can neither feel nor see the rain, while in it, knows neither wet nor dry."

She meant that she would have to be like such an insensitive and unintelligent person not to recognize the intensity of the Third Queen's grief.

Emilia continued, "If you were the masterpiece of some painter, I would buy you to instruct me for when I need to depict the greatest grief — indeed, yours is a heart-pierced demonstration of the greatest grief.

"But, alas, since you are a natural sister of our sex, a real woman rather than an artistic depiction of a woman, your sorrow beats so ardently upon me that it shall reflect from me and go to my brother-in-law's heart and warm it to feel some pity for you, even if his heart were made of stone. Please feel good comfort."

Theseus came forward and said, "Let's go to the temple. We will leave out not even a tiny portion of the sacred ceremony."

The First Queen said, "Oh, this celebration will longer last and will be more costly than the war that we, your suppliants, are asking you to fight. Remember that your fame resounds in the ear of the world. What you do quickly is not done rashly; your first thought is worth more than others' hard thinking, and your premeditation is worth more than their actions.

"But, by Jove, your actions, as soon as they move, subdue before they touch, just as ospreys do to the fish."

This society believed that ospreys fascinated fish: The fish would turn their bellies to the osprey and allow themselves to be caught.

The First Queen continued, "Think, dear Duke of Athens, think what beds our slain Kings have!"

The beds were the ground of the battlefield, which lay exposed to the elements.

The Second Queen said, "What griefs have our beds because our dear lords have none!"

"They have no beds fit for the dead," the Third Queen said, "Those who kill themselves with ropes for hanging, knives, drams of poison, or high places from which to throw themselves, those who are weary of this world's light, those who have to themselves been death's most horrid agents, are still allowed to have dust and shadow — graves — by human grace and mercy."

The First Queen said, "But our lords lie blistering underneath the visitating Sun, which visits their corpses the way a plague visits a house of people even though our lords were good Kings when they were living."

Theseus said, "That is true, and I will give you comfort by giving your dead husbands graves. To do that, I must make some work — fight a war — against Creon."

The First Queen said, "And that work presents itself to the doing. It must be done quickly. Now it will take form; the heat is gone tomorrow. Then, unprofitable toil must recompense itself with its own sweat."

Heated metal can be formed into shapes, but once the metal cools, it is no longer malleable. This is expressed in the proverb "Strike [with a blacksmith's hammer] while the iron's [metal's] hot."

The First Queen continued, "Now Creon, King of Thebes, thinks that he is secure and he will not be attacked. He does not dream that we three Queens stand before your powerful presence, rinsing with tears our holy begging in our eyes to make our petition clear. Our tears purify our supplication to you, and they make clear why we are supplicating you."

The Second Queen said, "Now you may conquer Creon, while he is drunk with his victory."

The Third Queen added, "And while his army is full of food and sloth."

Theseus said, "Artesius, you who best know how to select, suitable to this enterprise, the best soldiers for this proceeding, and the number of soldiers adequate to fight such a war, go forth and levy our worthiest soldiers while we dispatch this grand act of our life, this daring deed of fate in wedlock."

While Artesius was drafting good soldiers to fight against Thebes, Theseus intended to finish getting married.

The First Queen said to the other two Queens, "Dowagers, join hands. Let us be widows to our woes — we will feel the woes of widows. Delay commends us to a famishing hope. Because Theseus is delaying attacking Thebes, our hope that our husbands will be honorably buried diminishes."

All the Queens said to Theseus, "Farewell."

The Second Queen said, "We come unseasonably — at a bad time — but when could grief select, as judgment that is free from torment can, the fittest time to best solicit help?"

Theseus said, "Why, good ladies, this wedding to which I am going is greater and more important than any war. It more concerns me and is more important to me than all the actions that I have previously done or will in the future face."

The First Queen said, "This is making it all the more clear that our suit to you shall be neglected when her arms, which are able to keep Jove away from a council of the gods, shall by permission-granting moonlight enclose you tightly like a corslet, aka defensive armor."

The three Queens were afraid that Theseus, rather than making war against Creon, would preoccupy himself in making love to his bride, Hippolyta. In Book 14 of Homer's *Iliad*, Hera, wife of Zeus, King of the gods, whom the Romans knew as Jupiter or Jove (the Romans knew Hera as Juno), seduced him so that he would not pay attention to what was going on in the Trojan War. Because Hera did that, the Greeks were able to rally and fight well against the Trojans, whom at the time Zeus was helping.

The First Queen added, "Oh, when Hippolyta's twinning cherries — cherry-red lips — shall let their sweetness fall upon your tasteful lips, will you be thinking of rotting Kings or crying Queens? What care will you have for what you don't feel, when what you feel is able to make Mars spurn his drum? Even Mars, god of war, prefers having sex to fighting in a war.

"Oh, if you spend but one night in bed with her, every hour in it will make you hostage for a hundred more hours, and you shall remember nothing more than what that banquet bids you to remember. You will forget the war we request that you fight, and you will remember only the joys of sleeping with Hippolyta."

Hippolyta said to Theseus, "Although I think that it is very unlikely you should be so transported by the joys of bedding me that you will forget your promise to help these three widows, and although I am very sorry that I should be such a suitor, yet I think that if I did not, by the abstaining of the joy I would have in bed on our wedding night — for which abstinence breeds a deeper longing — cure their sickness brought on by an excess of grief that craves an immediate medicine, I should make all ladies think I am acting scandalously."

She knelt and continued, "Therefore, sir, as I shall here make trial of my entreaties to you, either presuming them to have some force, or concluding forever that they will always be as ineffectual as if I had not made them, postpone this business we are going about, and hang your shield before your heart — about that neck which is my possession, and which I freely lend to do these poor Queens service. I request that you postpone our wedding night and instead first help these three widowed Queens."

All three Queens said to Emilia, "Oh, help us now! Our cause cries for you to bend your knees and entreat Theseus to help us."

Emilia knelt and said to Theseus, "If you don't grant my sister her petition with the same vigor and with the same quickness and passion with which she makes her petition, from henceforth I'll not dare to ask you anything, nor be so foolhardy as ever to take a husband."

Theseus said, "Please stand up."

Hippolyta and Emilia rose.

Theseus then said, "I am entreating myself to do that which you kneel to request me to do."

He ordered, "Pirithous, lead on the bride; go and pray to the gods for success in and return from the war. Don't omit anything in the intended celebration.

"Queens, follow me, your soldier.

"Artesius, as I ordered you previously, go hence and at the shores of Aulis in Boeotia meet us with the forces you can raise. In Aulis, we shall find already assembled part of a number of troops for a business expected to be bigger than the war against Thebes."

Artesius exited.

Theseus kissed Hippolyta and said, "Since our main concern is haste, I stamp this kiss upon your red-as-a-currant lip. Sweetheart, keep this kiss as my token."

He then said to the wedding procession, "Go forward, for I will see you gone."

The wedding procession began to exit towards the temple.

Theseus said to Emilia, "Farewell, my beauteous sister-in-law."

He added, "Pirithous, fully keep the wedding feast. Don't omit even an hour of it."

Pirithous replied, "Sir, I'll follow you at your heels; I will go with you to Thebes. The celebratory feast shall wait until your return."

Theseus replied, "Fellow noble, I order you not to leave Athens. We shall be returning before you can end this feast, of which I ask you to make no abatement. I expect this war to be over quickly.

"Once more, farewell, all."

The wedding would occur, but it would be a wedding by proxy. Theseus would not be present.

Everyone except Theseus and the three Queens exited.

The First Queen said to Theseus, "Thus you always make good what good things the tongues of the world say about you."

The Second Queen said to Theseus, "And you earn a deity equal to that of Mars."

"If not above him," the Third Queen said, "for you, being only mortal, make your passions bend and submit to godlike honors; the gods themselves, some say, groan under such a mastery. Even the gods find it difficult to control their passions."

Theseus replied, "As we are men, thus should we do; once overcome by passions, we lose our title of being humans. Be of good cheer, ladies."

Using the royal plural, he said, "Now we turn towards obtaining your comforts."

Palamon and Arcite talked together in Thebes. They were first cousins, and Creon, King of Thebes, was their uncle.

Arcite said, "Dear Palamon, you are dearer in love and friendship to me than you are in blood relationship. You are my favorite cousin, and you are as yet unhardened in the sins of human nature. Let us leave the city of Thebes, and the temptations in it, before we further sully our gloss of youth. Here in Thebes we are as ashamed to abstain from sin as in other cities we would be ashamed to sin. To not swim with the current is almost to sink in the water; not swimming with the current at least takes an effort that diverts energy from and frustrates striving to do good. And if we follow the common stream in Thebes, it would bring us to a whirlpool where we would either spin around or drown; if we labor through the eddy, our gain is only life and weakness caused by our struggle."

Palamon replied, "Your advice is supported by examples. What strange ruins of human beings, since we first went to school, may we perceive walking in Thebes! Scars and poor clothing are the reward of the soldiers, the followers of Mars, god of war. Each soldier proposed as a goal for his bold efforts honor and golden ingots. Although the soldier fought well and won the battle, he did not receive honor and golden ingots, and now he is mocked by the peace for which he fought. Who then shall give offerings to Mars' so-scorned altar? I bleed pity when I meet such soldiers, and I wish great Juno would resume her ancient fit of jealousy to get the soldier work."

Juno is a jealous goddess who is capable of great hatred. She once lost a beauty contest and forever hated the city from which the judge of the contest came. The story is that Juno, Minerva, and Venus competed for a golden apple on which were inscribed the words "For the most beautiful." Paris, Prince of Troy, chose Venus. During the Trojan War, Venus supported Troy, while Juno and Minerva supported the attacking Greeks.

Juno also hated Thebes because her husband, Jupiter, King of the gods, had slept with and had sons by two mortal women associated with Thebes: Semele, who gave birth to the god Bacchus, and Alcmene, who gave birth to Hercules.

Palamon continued, "If Juno were to do that, then peace would be purged with blood to get rid of her soft, easy ways, and retain anew her charitable heart, which is now hard and harsher than strife or war could be."

This society believed that a long period of peace was bad and that it was good to have a war once in a while. It believed in this cycle: peace leads to plenty, then pride, then envy, then war, then poverty, then peace again. Peace leads to overeating, which is unhealthy.

This society also believed that blood-letting was necessary to cure many kinds of illness. Physicians would make a cut and allow their patients to bleed.

Arcite said, "Are you leaving something out? Do you meet no ruined people except the soldiers in the winding paths and twisting streets of Thebes? You began your speech as if you met decaying people of many kinds. Do you perceive none who arouse your pity except the disrespected soldier?"

Palamon replied, "Yes, I pity decaying humans wherever I find them, but I pity most those decaying humans who, sweating in an honorable toil, are paid with ice to cool them."

"It is not this I began to speak about," Arcite said. "The proper consideration of soldiers is a virtue that is not respected in Thebes. I was speaking of Thebes — how dangerous, if we want to keep our honors, it is for our residing. In Thebes every evil has a good appearance, and in Thebes everything that seems good is in reality evil. In Thebes, not to be exactly as the Thebans are is to be regarded as a foreigner, and in Thebes, foreigners are regarded as utter monsters."

Palamon said, "It is in our power — unless we fear being regarded as utter monsters and fear what apers and imitators can teach us — to be masters of our manners and morals. Why do I need to imitate another person's manner of acting, which is not contagious where there is faith?

"And why do I need to be fond of another person's way of speaking, when by using my own speech I may be reasonably understood — and saved, too, if I speak it truthfully? Why am I bound by any obligation of a nobleman to follow a nobleman who follows his tailor, perhaps as long until the followed make pursuit — the tailor chases the nobleman because the nobleman has not paid his bill? Why should I follow the advice of a tailor and spend all my money on clothing?

"And let me know why my own barber is unblessed, and with him my poor chin, too, because it is not scissored in such a way that it is the exact imitation of the chin of a favorite celebrity? What canon — law — is there that commands me to take my rapier from my hip so that I can show off by dangling it in my hand, or to show off by walking on tiptoe before the street is foul with mud? Either I am the forehorse in the team of horses, or I am none of the horses in the train of horses that follow and draw the carriage or wagon. I am not a follower; I am the first, I am the leader, or I am nothing.

"Still, these poor slight sores I have been talking about don't need a bandage. That which rips my bosom almost to the heart is —"

Arcite finished the sentence: "— our Uncle Creon."

"Yes, he," Palamon said. "Creon is a most unrestrained tyrant, whose successes make people unafraid of Heaven and assure villainous people that beyond the power of evil there's nothing. He almost makes faith ill and feverous, and the only thing he deifies is changeable fortune. He gives credit to himself alone for the capabilities of those who serve him; what they accomplish he credits to his own strength and actions.

"Creon commands men to serve him, and he commands — takes for himself — what they win in doing that service: profit and glory. He is a man who is not afraid to do harm, but he dares not do good.

"Let the blood of mine that's related to him be sucked from me by leeches; let the leeches break and fall off me when they are filled with that corrupted blood."

Arcite said, "Clear-spirited cousin, let's leave Creon's court, so that we may share nothing of his widely famous infamy because our metaphorical milk will taste of the pasture in which we reside, and we must be either vile or disobedient."

When cows eat onions, their milk tastes like onions.

He continued, "We must not be Creon's kinsmen in blood with the exception that we are all noblemen in quality."

"Nothing is truer," Palamon said. "I think the echoes of his shames have deafened the ears of Heavenly justice. The cries of widows descend again into their throats and are not heard by the gods."

Valerius arrived.

Palamon greeted him: "Valerius."

Valerius said, "The King calls for both of you, but be leaden-footed and slow to arrive until his great rage stops riding his back. Phoebus Apollo, when he broke his whip handle and exclaimed against the horses of the Sun, only whispered in comparison with the loudness of Creon's fury."

Phoebus Apollo had allowed his son Phaëthon to drive the chariot of the Sun across the sky. Being mortal, Phaëthon was unable to control the immortal horses that drew the chariot, and so the Sun careened wildly across the sky and came so close to the Earth that it was in danger of burning up. Jupiter saved the Earth and all its inhabitants by throwing a thunderbolt that killed Phaëthon. Phoebus Apollo was angry at the death of his son and took out his anger on his immortal horses.

Palamon said, "Small winds shake Creon. But what's the matter?"

Valerius replied, "Theseus, who appalls where and when he threatens, has sent deadly defiance to Creon and pronounces a sentence of ruin to Thebes, and he is at hand to seal with his actions the promise of his wrath. Theseus is ready and at hand to make war against Creon and Thebes."

"Let him approach," Arcite said. "Except that we fear the gods whom he serves, he causes not a jot of terror to us. Yet what man would reduce his own worth to a third — such is the case for both Palamon and me — when it's the case that his action is made cloudy with dregs because his mind is assured that what he goes about doing is bad? When a soldier knows that he is fighting for a bad leader, that knowledge greatly reduces the soldier's effectiveness."

"Don't think about that," Palamon said. "Our services stand now for Thebes, not Creon. We are fighting for our city, not for our King. Yet to be neutral to Creon would be dishonorable, and it would be rebellious to oppose him. Therefore, we must stand with him to the mercy of our fate, which has set the time for our last minute of life."

"So we must," Arcite said.

He then said to Valerius, "Is it said this war's already afoot? Or, is it the case that a war will occur if Thebes fails to meet some condition?"

"The war is in motion," Valerius said. "The intelligence of state came in the same instant as the defier did. Theseus and the declaration of war came at the same time. Fighting will take place."

Palamon said, "Let's go to King Creon, who, if he had even a quarter of the honor that his enemy Theseus has, the blood we risk would be for our health.

The blood would be not spent wastefully, but instead it would be invested to purchase honor. But alas, since our hands are advanced before our hearts, and since we are fighting on behalf of a King whom we do not respect, to what will the fall of the stroke of the enemy's sword do damage? If we fight in an honorable cause, we gain honor. What do we risk by fighting for this particular cause?"

Arcite said, "Let the war's outcome, that never-erring arbitrator, tell us when we ourselves know all, and let us follow the beckoning of our fortune. Whatever will be, will be; it has been fated. When we know the outcome of the war, we will know what fate has decreed."

— 1.3 —

Hippolyta and Emilia had traveled a distance with Pirithous, but now they had to say goodbye to him. He was traveling to join Theseus at Thebes. The war against Thebes was taking longer than Theseus had said it would.

"Go no further with me," Pirithous said.

"Sir, farewell," Hippolyta said. "Repeat my wishes to our great lord, of whose success I dare not have any doubt, yet I wish him an excess and overflow of power, if it is possible, to endure ill-dealing fortune. May success speed to him. An abundance never hurts good governors. Theseus can manage well an abundance of soldiers."

Pirithous replied, "Although I know that Theseus' ocean does not need my poor drops, yet they must yield their tribute there. I want to join him and fight in the war."

He then said to Emilia, "My precious maiden, those best emotions and feelings that the Heavens infuse in their most skillfully crafted pieces, keep enthroned in your dear heart!"

"Thanks, sir," Emilia replied. "Remember me to our all-royal brother-in-law, for whose success the great Bellona, Roman goddess of war, I'll solicit, and since in our Earthly state petitions are not understood without gifts to encourage their reception, I'll offer to her what I shall be advised she likes. Our hearts are in his army, in his tent."

Hippolyta said, "And in his bosom. We are Amazons, we have been soldiers, and we cannot weep when our friends don their helmets or put out on the dangerous sea, or tell about babes spitted on the lance, or women who have boiled their infants in — and afterward ate them — the briny salt tears they wept as they killed them."

Such things happen. 2 Kings 6:28-29 tells this about a famine in Samaria:

28 Also the king said unto her, What aileth thee? And she answered, This woman said unto me, Give thy son that we may eat him today, and we will eat my son tomorrow,

29 So we sod [boiled] my son, and did eat him: and I said to her the day after, Give thy son, that we may eat him, but she hath hid her son. (1599 Geneva Bible)

Lamentations 4:10 states, "*The hands of the pitiful women have sodden [boiled] their own children, which were their meat in the destruction of the daughter of my people*" (1599 Geneva Bible).

In addition, Josephus' *History of the Jewish War* tells of a mother who ate her son's flesh during the famine that occurred at a time when Jerusalem was besieged:

"[...] *and it was now become impossible for her any way to find any more food, while the famine pierced through her very bowels and marrow, when also her passion was fired to a degree beyond the famine itself; nor did she consult with any thing but with her passion and the necessity she was in. She then attempted a most unnatural thing; and snatching up her son, who was a child sucking at her breast, she said, 'O thou miserable infant! for whom shall I preserve thee in this war, this famine, and this sedition? As to the war with the Romans, if they preserve our lives, we must be slaves. This famine also will destroy us, even before that slavery comes upon us. Yet are these seditious rogues more terrible than both the other. Come on; be thou my food, and be thou a fury to these seditious varlets, and a by-word to the world, which is all that is now wanting to complete the calamities of us Jews.' As soon as she had said this, she slew her son, and then roasted him, and eat the one half of him, and kept the other half by her concealed.*" (Source: Flavius Josephus. *The Works of Flavius Josephus.* Translated by William Whiston. A.M. Auburn and Buffalo, NY: John E. Beardsley, 1895.)

Hippolyta added, "So if you stay then to see in us women who stay at home and do household chores and know nothing of the acts of war, we would hold you here forever because Emilia and I will never be such women."

"May peace be to you as I pursue this war," Pirithous said. "That way, when the war is won, peace will already be yours."

Pirithous exited.

Emilia said, "How his longing follows his friend! Since Theseus' departure, although Pirithous' sports and games needed his seriousness and skill, he has played them carelessly and without paying much attention to them. Neither gain made him regard, or loss consider, his sports and games. Instead, his hands played sports and games, while his head thought about being with Theseus. He was like a nurse taking care of two very different twins. Have you observed him since our great lord Theseus departed?"

"Very carefully," Hippolyta replied, "and I loved him for it. Theseus and Pirithous have taken shelter in many as dangerous and as poor a corner in which peril and poverty contended to see which was worse. They have gone in skiffs over torrents whose roaring tyranny and power in the slightest measure of either of these was dreadful, and they have fought out together where Death's self was lodged. They visited Hell itself, yet fate brought them safely away. Their knot of love, tied, weaved, entangled, with a finger so true, so long, and of so deep a cunning, may be worn out in death, but can be never undone in life.

"I think Theseus cannot be an umpire to himself, cleaving his conscience into two sides and doing each side equal and impartial justice — he loves justice best. Theseus divides his conscience in his consideration of Pirithous, who is his second self, and himself, and he cannot decide whom he loves best."

Emilia said, "Doubtless there is a one he loves best, and reason has no manners if it says that one is not you.

"I was acquainted once with a time when I enjoyed a playfellow. You were at the wars when she died and enriched the grave. She made the bed — the grave — too proud. She took leave of the Moon, which then looked pale at parting, when our count of years was each eleven. With her death, she stopped serving Diana, goddess of the Moon and protector of virgins."

"She was Flavina," Hippolyta said.

"Yes," Emilia said. "You talk of Pirithous' and Theseus' love. Theirs has more ground and a firmer foundation, is more maturely seasoned, and is more held together with strong judgment, and the one of the other may be said to water their intertangled roots of love and to meet each other's needs.

"But I and the playfellow I sigh about now and spoke of were innocent things.

"We loved each other just because we did, and like the elements that know neither what nor why, yet effect striking and exceptional outcomes through their operation, our souls did so to one another.

"What she liked was then by me approved and what she did not like was then by me condemned without any further consideration.

"The flower that I would pluck and put between my breasts — then but beginning to swell about the nipple — she would long for until she had one like it, and put it in her similarly innocent cradle, where, like the mythic Phoenix that immolates itself on a bier of fragrant wood, the flowers died in the midst of perfume.

"On my head no decorative trinket appeared without her wanting one like it. Her taste in clothing — pretty, although perhaps what she wore was carelessly put on — I followed when I most carefully dressed myself.

"When my ear had stolen some new melody, or randomly I hummed one of my coinage, why, it was a note on which her spirits would sojourn — rather, dwell on — and she would sing it in her sleep.

"This account of my childhood friend and our love for each other — which 'fury' every innocent child knows well — is a poor account of the original events that were of great importance."

"Fury" can mean strong passion, including strong sexual passion.

Emilia and Flavina were innocent playmates who deeply loved each other. Because they were so innocent, their love did not suffer from such adult feelings as strong sexual passion and jealousy.

Strong sexual passion can cause jealousy even between lifelong friends, as it would between Palamon and Arcite, but the love between Emilia and Flavina had none of that.

Emilia continued, "My account of this friendship between Flavina and me has this conclusion: The true love between maiden and maiden may be more than in sex dividual."

In other words, "The true love between maiden and maiden may be more than the love shared by a man and a woman."

If something is dividual, it is separate and distinct, and it can be separated. A man and a woman are different.

Emilia believed that the true love between two virgin females may be more than the true love found in a heterosexual couple.

Hippolyta replied, "You're out of breath, and this high-speeded pace of your speech is only to say that you shall never — like the maid Flavina — love any who is called a man."

"I am sure I shall not," Emilia said.

Hippolyta said, "Now, unfortunately, weak sister, I must no more believe you in this point — although I know that you yourself believe this point — than I will trust a sickly appetite, which loathes even as it longs.

"But to be sure, my sister, if I were receptive to your persuasion, you have said enough to shake me from the arm of the all-noble Theseus, for whose fortunes I will now go in and kneel and pray for, with great assurance that I, more than his Pirithous, possess the high throne in his heart."

"I am not against your faith, yet I continue to believe my faith," Emilia said.

Cornets sounded, along with the many noises of a battle. The call for a retreat sounded.

Theseus, the victor of the battle and of the war against Thebes, arrived, as did the three widowed Queens, who met him and fell on their faces before him. Many lords and soldiers were present.

The First Queen said, "May no planet be malignant to you!"

This society, which believed in astrology, thought that planets could have a beneficial or a malignant influence on people.

The Second Queen said, "May both Heaven and Earth befriend you forever."

The Third Queen said, "I cry 'Amen' to all the good that may be wished upon your head."

Theseus replied, "The impartial gods, who from the high Heavens view us, their mortal herd, behold those who sin and, at the time the gods think right, chastise the sinners. Thus the impartial gods have chastised the Thebans."

He said to the three Queens, "Go and find the bones of your dead lords and honor them with a treble ceremony. Rather than a gap should appear in their dear rites, we would fill the gap, but we will depute men who shall invest you in your dignities and make right each thing my haste to return to Athens leaves imperfect.

"So, Queens, *adieu*, and may Heaven's good eyes look on you."

The three Queens exited.

A herald and some soldiers bearing on biers the badly wounded Palamon and Arcite entered the scene. Palamon and Arcite were expected to die soon.

Seeing Palamon and Arcite, Theseus asked, "Who are those men?"

The herald answered, "They are men of great quality and high rank, as may be judged by their armor and equipment. Some men of Thebes have told us that these two men are sisters' children and nephews to the King."

Recognizing the two prisoners, Theseus said, "By the helmet of Mars, I saw them in the war, similar to a pair of lions and smeared with the blood of their prey, make open lanes into the aghast troops opposing them. I fixed my notice constantly on them, for they were a sight worth a god's view. What was it that prisoner told me when I enquired their names?"

Theseus had been impressed by the military skill of Palamon and Arcite and had earlier asked a prisoner for their names.

The herald replied, "With your leave, they're called Arcite and Palamon."

"That's right," Theseus said. "Those are the names. They are not dead?"

"Nor are they in a state of life," the herald said. "Had they been taken prisoner when their last hurts were given, it is possible that they might have recovered. Yet they breathe and still have the name of men rather than corpses."

"Then treat them like men," Theseus said. "The very dregs of such men exceed the wine of others by millions of times. Assemble all our physicians in their behalf. Don't be niggard with our most expensive balms; instead, use them lavishly. Their lives concern us much more than Thebes' worth.

"Rather than have them freed of this plight, and in their morning state — alive, healthy, hostile to us, sound, and at liberty — I would prefer them to be dead."

Using the royal plural, Theseus continued, "But forty thousand times we would rather have them prisoners to us than to Death. Bear them speedily from our kind air, which to wounded men like them is unkind, and minister to them what man to man may do."

This society believed that open air was bad for wounds.

Still using the royal plural, Theseus continued, "For our sake, do more than what man to man may do.

"I have known frights, fury, friends' behests, love's provocations, zeal, a mistress' task, desire for liberty, a fever, and madness to each set a target that human nature could not reach without some imposition; in such cases, sickness in will has over-wrestled strength in reason. Strongly motivated men are capable of achieving much more than cold reason says they are capable of achieving."

This is true, and not just of men. Mothers have performed incredible acts of strength in order to save their children.

Theseus continued, "For our love and the great healer-god Apollo's mercy, have our best physicians use their best skill to heal these men."

Using the royal plural, he then ordered, "Take these men into the city of Thebes. From there, once we have organized disorganized matters, we will speed to Athens before our army goes there."

The Queens had located the corpses of their husbands and had given orders for them to be placed in coffins. The Queens now sang a dirge:

"Urns and odors bring away;
"Vapors, sighs, darken the day;
"Our dole [sorrow] more deadly looks than dying;
"Balms and gums and heavy cheers [sad faces],
"Sacred vials filled with tears,
"And clamors through the wild air flying.
"Come, all sad and solemn shows
"That are quick-eyed [keen-eyed] Pleasure's foes;
"We convent [call together] naught [nothing] else but woes.
"We convent [call together] naught [nothing] else but woes."

The Third Queen said to the Second Queen, "This funeral path takes you to your household's grave. May joy be yours again; may peace sleep with him."

The Second Queen said to the First Queen, "And this path will take you to your household, where you will bury your husband."

The First Queen said to the Third Queen, "Your path is this way. The Heavens lend a thousand differing ways to one sure end. A thousand paths lead to death and the grave."

The Third Queen said, "This world's a city full of wandering streets, and death's the marketplace where each one meets."

Many cities had many streets leading to the marketplace.

CHAPTER 2
— 2.1 —

The jailor was talking to a wooer — a man who was wooing the jailor's young daughter. They were in a garden that the jail overlooked.

The jailor said, "I may give you little wealth while I live; I may give something to you, but not much. Unfortunately, the prison I keep, although it is for great ones, yet great ones seldom come; before one salmon you shall take a number of minnows."

Wealthy prisoners paid the jailor extra for better food and accommodations. This was a way for the jailor to supplement his income.

The jailor continued, "I am rumored to be wealthier than I have reason to believe that the rumor is truthful. I wish that I really were as wealthy as I am rumored to be. But by the Virgin Mary, I say that what I have, be it what it will, I will leave to my daughter at the day of my death."

The wooer replied, "Sir, I demand no more than your own offer, and I will endow your daughter with what I have promised."

"Well, we will talk more about this when the wedding is past. But do you have a definite promise from her that she will marry you? When I see that to be true, then I will give you my consent to marry her."

The jailer's daughter, carrying rushes, arrived. The rushes served as floor coverings for the prisoners.

The wooer said, "I have her promise, sir. Here she comes."

The jailer said to his daughter, "Your friend and I have chanced to talk about you here, concerning the old business. But no more of that now; as soon as the court commotion is over, we will have an end of it. In the meantime, look carefully after the two prisoners. I can tell you they are Princes."

"These rushes are for their chamber," the jailer's daughter said. "It is a pity they are in prison, and it would be a pity if they should be out of prison. I think they have the patience to make any adversity ashamed. The prison itself is proud of them, and they have all of the world in their chamber. Many people visit them."

"They are reputed to be a pair of absolute men," the jailer said.

"Truly, I think the rumor speaks only inadequately about them. They stand a step above what is reported about them."

"I heard it said about them that in the battle they were the outstanding soldiers," the jailer said.

"That is very likely, for they are noble sufferers," the jailor's daughter said. "I marvel at how they would have looked had they been victors. With their constant nobility, they make a freedom out of bondage, making misery their mirth and making affliction a trifle to jest at."

"Do they?" the jailer asked.

"It seems to me that they have no more perception of their captivity than I of ruling Athens," the jailer's daughter replied. "They eat well, look merrily, talk of many things, but say nothing about their own captivity and disasters. Yet sometimes a broken sigh, martyred as it were in the deliverance, will break from one of them — and then the other immediately gives it so sweet a rebuke that I could wish myself a sigh to be so scolded, or at least a sigher to be comforted."

"I never saw them," the wooer said.

"Duke Theseus himself came privately in the night, and he brought them," the jailer said.

Palamon and Arcite, in shackles, appeared at the window of the jail.

The jailer continued, "What the reason for it is, I don't know. Look, yonder they are; that's Arcite looking out of the window."

"No, sir, no, that's Palamon," the jailer's daughter said. "Arcite is the shorter of the two; you may perceive a part of him through the window."

"Stop your pointing," the jailer said. "They would not point at us. Let's get out of their sight."

"It is a holiday to look at them," the jailer's daughter said. "Lord, the difference of men!"

Yes, men are different from women.

The jailer, his daughter, and the wooer exited.

Palamon and Arcite talked near the window of the jail cell.

Palamon asked, "How are you, noble cousin?"

"How are you, sir?" Arcite replied.

"Why, I am strong enough to laugh at misery and endure the fortune of war, yet I am afraid that we are prisoners forever, cousin."

"I believe it, and I have resolved to patiently accept my fate as a prisoner and have put aside my future."

"Oh, cousin Arcite, where is Thebes now? Where is our noble country? Where are our friends and families? Never more must we behold those comforts, never more see the hardy youths strive for the games of honor, displaying the brightly colored favors of their ladies like tall ships under sail, then start amongst them and like an east wind leave them all behind us like lazy clouds, while we, Palamon and Arcite, in the time it would take to wag a playful leg, outstripped the people's praises and won the garlands before the people had time to wish them ours.

"Oh, never more shall we two exercise, like twins of honor, our arms and weapons in battle again, and feel our fiery horses like proud seas under us. Our good swords now — Mars, the red-eyed god of war, never wore better — torn from our sides, like age must run to rust and adorn the temples of those gods who hate us. These hands shall never more draw them out like lightning to blast whole armies."

The victor sometimes dedicated the weapons of defeated enemies to a temple of a god.

Arcite replied, "No, Palamon, those hopes of free exercise are prisoners with us. Here we are and here the graces of our youths must wither like a too-early spring."

The first warm day or two following winter is usually succeeded by one or more cold days.

Arcite continued, "Here old age must find us and — which is heaviest and most sorrowful, Palamon — must find us unmarried. The sweet embraces of a loving wife, loaded with kisses, armed with a thousand Cupids, shall never clasp our necks. No children of ours will be born and know us — no tiny figures of ourselves shall we ever see, to gladden our old age. We will never teach them like young eagles to gaze boldly at bright armor and we will never say, 'Remember what your fathers were, and conquer!'"

This society believed that eagles taught their young to gaze directly at the Sun.

Arcite continued, "The fair-eyed maidens shall weep about our banishments and in their songs curse ever-blind Lady Fortune until she for shame sees what a wrong she has done to youth and nature.

"This prison is all our world. We shall know nothing here but one another, and we shall hear nothing but the clock that tells our woes. The vine shall grow, but we shall never see it. Summer shall come, and with her all delights, but dead-cold winter must inhabit here always."

"That is too true, Arcite," Palamon said. "To our Theban hounds that shook the aged forest with their echoes no more now must we halloo; no more must we shake our pointed javelins while the angry swine flies like a Parthian quiver from our rages, with its back struck with our well-steeled arrows."

The swine's back would have so many arrows sticking out of it that it would look like the quiver full of arrows belonging to an archer of Parthia.

Palamon added, "All valiant activities, the food and nourishment of noble minds, in us two here shall perish. We shall die as children of grief and ignorance — which is the curse of honor."

"Yet, cousin," Arcite said, "even from the bottom of these miseries, from all these miseries that bad fortune can inflict upon us, I see two comforts rising, two complete blessings, if the gods please: first, to hold here a brave patience and bravely accept our fate, and second, the enjoying of our griefs together.

"While Palamon is with me, let me perish if I think this is our prison!"

"Certainly it is a major goodness, cousin, that our fortunes were entwined together," Palamon said. "It is very true: Even if two souls who have been put in two noble bodies suffer the bitterness of fate, as long as they grow together, will never sink; they must not, even if they could. A willing man dies sleeping and all's done — a man who accepts death dies as easily as if he were sleeping."

Arcite asked, "Shall we make worthy uses of this place — this prison — that all men hate so much?"

"How, gentle cousin?" Palamon asked.

"Let's think this prison is a holy sanctuary that will keep us from the corruption of worse men. We are young and still desire the ways of honor that liberty and common conversation, the poison to pure spirits, might similar to women woo us to wander from. What worthy blessing can exist but our imaginations may make it ours? And here, being thus together, we are an endless mine of wealth to one another. We are one another's wife, ever begetting new births of love. We are father, friends, and acquaintances. We are, in one another, families. I am your heir, and you are mine. This place is our inheritance; no hard oppressor dares take this from us; here with a little patience we shall live long and loving. No excesses seek us. The hand of war hurts none here, nor do the seas swallow their youth. Were we at liberty, a wife might part us lawfully, or business might part us. Quarrels might consume us. The malice of ill men might crave our acquaintance. I might sicken, cousin, where you should never know it, and so perish without your noble hand to close my eyes, and without your prayers to the gods. A thousand events, if we were away from here, could sever us."

"You have made me — I thank you, cousin Arcite — almost delighted with my captivity. What a misery it is to live abroad and everywhere! It is a life like that of a beast, I think. I find the court here, I am sure, more content than any court elsewhere, and all those pleasures that woo the wills of men to vanity I see through now, and I am able to tell the world that it is only a gaudy shadow that old Time takes with him as he passes by.

"What would we be, if we were to grow old in the court of Creon, the court where sin is justice, and lust and ignorance are the virtues of the great ones? Cousin Arcite, if the loving gods had not found this place for us, we would have died as Creon's courtiers do — they are ill old men, unwept, and with the people's curses as their epitaphs. Shall I say more?"

"I want to hear you speak more."

"You shall. Is there any record of any two who loved each other as friends better than we do, Arcite?"

"Surely there cannot be."

"I do not think it possible that our friendship should ever leave us," Palamon said.

"Until our deaths occur, it cannot," Arcite said.

Emilia and her female attendant entered the garden below the prison window.

Arcite continued, "And after our death our spirits shall be led to those who love eternally in Elysium."

Palamon caught sight of Emilia and stared at her, silent.

Arcite said, "Speak on, sir."

Emilia said to her female attendant, "This garden has a world of pleasures in it. What flower is this?"

"It is called narcissus, madam."

In mythology, Narcissus was a handsome boy who fell in love with his reflection in a stream.

"Narcissus was certainly a fair boy, but a fool to love himself," Emilia said. "Weren't there maidens enough for him to find someone to love?"

Arcite said to Palamon, "Please, continue to speak."

Palamon replied, "Yes."

Emilia said to her female attendant, "Or were all the maidens hard-hearted?"

"They could not be to one as good-looking as Narcissus."

"You would not be hard-hearted to him," Emilia said.

"I think I should not, madam."

"That's a good girl. But take heed about your kindness, though."

"Why, madam?"

"Men are mad things," Emilia said.

More than one woman has found her kindness to be misinterpreted as leading a man on.

Arcite said to Palamon, "Will you continue what you were saying, cousin?"

Emilia said to her female servant, "Can you embroider such flowers in silk, girl?"

"Yes."

"I'll have a gown full of them, and of these other flowers. This is a pretty color. Won't it look splendid on a skirt, girl?"

"It will look beautiful, madam."

Arcite said, "Cousin, cousin! How are you, sir? Why, Palamon!"

"Never until now was I in prison, Arcite."

"Why, what's the matter, man?"

"Behold, and wonder!" Palamon replied. "By Heaven, she is a goddess."

Arcite looked at Emilia and said, "I see!"

"Kneel and pay homage to her. She is a goddess, Arcite."

Emilia said to her female attendant, "Of all flowers I think a rose is best."

"Why, gentle madam?"

"It is the very emblem of a maiden," Emilia said. "For when the west wind courts her gently, how modestly she blossoms and beautifies the Sun with her chaste blushes! When the rough and impatient north wind comes near her, then like chastity she locks her beauties in her bud again, and leaves him to base prickly thorns."

Emilia's female attendant said, "Yet, good madam, sometimes her modesty will blossom so far she falls for it."

A rose blossom can fall because of the way a rough and impatient north wind treats it; it withers and falls off the stem. A maiden who falls for the line of a rough and impatient man can fall in another way — she can fall into bed.

Emilia's female attendant added, "A maiden, if she has any honor, would be loath to take a rose as a model to follow."

"You are misinterpreting what I say as being wanton!" Emilia said.

Arcite said to Palamon, "She is wondrously beautiful."

"She is all the beauty that exists on Earth," Palamon replied.

Emilia said to her female attendant, "The Sun grows high. Let's walk in. Keep these flowers. We'll see how near art can come to their colors. I am wondrously merry-hearted. I could laugh now."

A proverb stated, "Laugh and lie down."

Her female attendant said, "I could lie down, I am sure."

"And take someone with you?" Emilia asked.

"That's as we bargain, madam," her female attendant answered.

It could happen.

Emilia said, "Well, agree then."

The two women exited from the garden.

"What do you think of this beauty?" Palamon asked Arcite.

"This beauty is a rare one."

"Is it only a rare one?"

Arcite answered, "She is a matchless beauty."

"Might not a man well lose himself and love her?" Palamon asked.

"I cannot tell what you have done," Arcite said, "but I have lost myself and I do love her, damn my eyes for it! Now I feel my shackles."

"You love her, then?"

"Who would not love her?"

"And desire her?"

"I want her more than I want my freedom," Arcite answered.

"I saw her first," Palamon said.

"That's nothing."

"But it shall be."

"I saw her, too," Arcite said.

"Yes, but you must not love her."

"I will not, as you do, love her to worship her as she is Heavenly and a blessed goddess. I love her as a woman, and I want to enjoy her. So both of us may love her."

The kind of enjoying he meant was enjoying her in bed.

"You shall not love her at all," Palamon said.

"Not love her at all! Who shall deny me?"

"I, who first saw her," Palamon said. "I, who took possession first with my eye of all those beauties in her revealed to mankind."

Palamon now began to use the less formal, less respectful pronouns "thou" and "thee" and "thy" to refer to Arcite, rather than the more formal, more respectful pronouns "you" and "your" that he had been using.

One might expect that Arcite and Palamon, who were both relatives and close friends, to regularly use the informal pronouns "thou" and "thee" to refer to each other, but they regularly used the pronoun "you." Sometimes, close friends can treat each other with excessive formality as a sign of respect.

He said to Arcite, "If thou love her, or entertain a hope to blight my wishes, thou art a traitor, Arcite, and a fellow as false as thy title to her. Friendship, blood relationship, and all the ties between us I disclaim if thou think once upon her."

"Yes, I love her," Arcite said, "and if the lives of all my family members lay on it, I must do so. I love her with my soul. If that will lose you, then farewell, Palamon. I say again, I love her, and in loving her I maintain I am as worthy and as free a lover and have as just a title to her beauty as any Palamon or anyone living who is a man's son."

"Have I called thee friend?" Palamon asked.

"Yes, and you have found me to be a friend," Arcite replied. "Why are you so moved? Let me reason coolly and calmly with you: Aren't I part of your blood, part of your soul? You have told me that I was Palamon and you were Arcite."

"Yes," Palamon said.

"Am I not liable to those emotions, those joys, griefs, angers, and fears that my friend shall experience?"

"You may be."

"Why then would you deal so cunningly, so strangely, so unlike a noble kinsman, to love alone? Speak truly, do you think me unworthy to look at her?"

"No," Palamon said, "but I think thee unjust if thou pursue that sight."

"Because another person first sees the enemy, shall I stand still and let my honor down, and never charge?"

"Yes, if the enemy is only one person," Palamon said.

"But say that one enemy would rather combat me?" Arcite asked.

In combat, one person could challenge an enemy to fight in single combat.

"Then let that one say so, and use thy freedom to do what thou wants. Else, if thou pursue her, be like that cursed man who hates his country — be a branded villain."

In the Middle Ages, a criminal could be punished by being branded.

"You are mad," Arcite said.

"I must be," Palamon said. "Until thou are worthy, Arcite, it concerns me. And in this madness if I put thee at risk and take thy life, I deal but truly."

"Damn, sir! You are acting exactly like a child. I will love her. I must, I ought to do so, and I dare, and all this justly."

"Oh, if now thy false self and thy friend — me, Palamon — had the good fortune to have one hour at liberty and grasp our good swords in our hands, I would quickly teach thee what it were to filch affection from another. Thou are baser in it than a pickpocket. Just put thy head a little more out of this window, and as I have a soul, I'll nail thy life to the window sash."

"Thou dare not, fool," Arcite said, beginning to use the less formal, less respectful pronouns that Palamon had been using. "Thou can not; thou are feeble. Put my head out? I'll throw my body out and leap into the garden when I see her next, and throw myself between her arms to anger thee."

The jailer arrived.

"Say no more," Palamon said. "The jailkeeper's coming. I shall live to knock thy brains out with my shackles."

"Do it! I dare thee!" Arcite said.

"By your leave, gentlemen," the jailer said respectfully.

"What is it, honest jailkeeper?" Palamon asked.

"Lord Arcite, you must immediately go to Theseus, the Duke of Athens. I don't yet know why."

"I am ready to go, jailkeeper," Arcite said.

"Prince Palamon, I must for awhile bereave you of your fair cousin's company," the jailer said.

Arcite and the jailer exited.

"And you can bereave me, too, whenever you please, of life," Palamon said to himself. "Why has Arcite been sent for? It may be he shall marry Emilia; he's a good-looking man, and likely enough the Duke has taken notice of both his noble blood and his noble body. But his falsehood! Why should a friend be treacherous? If that falsehood should get him a wife so noble and so fair, then let honest men never love again.

"Once more I would love to see this fair Emilia. Blessed garden and fruit and flowers more blessed that still blossom as her bright eyes shine on you, I wish I were, in exchange for all my future good fortune, yonder little tree, yonder blooming apricot! How I would spread and fling my wanton arms in at her window. I would bring her fruit fit for the gods to feed on. Youth and pleasure whenever she tasted should be doubled on her; and, if she be not Heavenly, I would make her so near the gods in nature that they should fear her."

The jailer returned.

Palamon continued, "And then I am sure she would love me."

Seeing the jailer, he said, "What is the news, jailkeeper? Where's Arcite?"

"He has been banished and ordered into exile," the jailer answered. "Prince Pirithous obtained Arcite's liberty, but never again upon his oath and life must Arcite set foot upon this Kingdom. Arcite has sworn an oath on his life that he will not return here."

"He's a blessed man," Palamon said. "He shall see Thebes again, and call to arms the bold young men who, when he orders them to charge, will fall on the enemy like fire. Arcite shall have a chance, if he dares to make himself a lover worthy of wooing her, yet in the field to fight a battle for her, and, if he loses her then, he's a passionless coward. How bravely may he bear himself to win her if he is noble Arcite — he has a thousand ways to win her!

"If I were at liberty, I would do things of such a virtuous greatness that this lady, this blushing virgin, should take manhood to her and seek to rape me."

The jailer said, "My lord, for you I have this charge, this order, to —"

Palamon said, "— to discharge my life?"

One meaning of the word "charge" was to load a firearm. The firearm could be discharged against Palamon and take his life.

The jailer replied, "No, but from this place to remove your Lordship. The windows are too open and easy to escape through."

"May the Devils take those who are so malicious to me!" Palamon said. "Please, kill me."

"And hang for it afterward!" the jailer said.

"By this good light, the Sun, I swear that if I had a sword I would kill thee."

"Why, my lord?" the jailer asked.

"Thou bring such paltry, scurvy news continually, that thou are not worthy of life. I will not go."

"Indeed you must, my lord," the jailer replied.

"Will I be able to see the garden from my new cell?" Palamon asked.

"No."

"Then I am determined that I will not go."

"I must force you to go then," the jailer said, "and, because you are dangerous, I'll clap more irons on you."

"Do, good jailkeeper," Palamon said. "I'll shake them so that you shall not sleep. I'll make you a new morris dance."

People performing a morris dance shook bells attached to their clothing. Palamon's new kind of morris dance would involve shaking his shackles.

Palamon asked, "Must I go?"

"There is no alternative. You must go."

"Farewell, kind window," Palamon said.

He now used "thee" and "thou" in their informal, affectionate meanings: "May a rude wind never hurt thee, kind window.

"Oh, my lady, if ever thou have felt what sorrow was, dream how I suffer.

"Come, jailer. You can now metaphorically bury me."

In the country outside Athens, Arcite, wearing an ordinary cloak that disguised his nobility, said to himself, "Am I banished from the Kingdom? It is a benefit, a mercy I must thank them for; but being banished from the free enjoying of that face I die for, oh, it was a carefully planned punishment, a worse death than could be imagined — such a vengeance that, were I old and wicked, all my sins could never pluck upon me. Palamon, thou have the advantage now; thou shall stay and see her bright eyes break like dawn each morning against thy window and let life into thee; thou shall feed upon the sweetness of a noble beauty that nature has never exceeded and never shall.

"Good gods, what happiness has Palamon! Twenty to one he'll come to a position where he can speak to her, and if she is as gentle and kind as she is fair, I know she'll be his. He has a tongue that will tame tempests and make the wild rocks frolic.

"Come what can come, the worst that can come is my death. I will not leave the Kingdom. I know my own Kingdom — Thebes — is only a heap of ruins, and I will get no help there. If I go away from Athens, Palamon will have her.

"I am resolved that another shape — a disguise — shall either make me or end my fortunes. Either way I will be happy. I'll see her and be near her, or I'll be no more — I'll be dead."

Five rustics arrived. The countryman in the lead carried a garland.

Arcite stepped aside.

The first countryman said, "My masters, I'll be there, that's certain."

The second countryman said, "And I'll be there."

The third countryman said, "And I will be there, too."

The fourth countryman said, "Why, then, I'll join you, boys. The worst that can happen to me is I'll get a talking-to. Let the plow play today; I'll whip the jades' tails tomorrow to make them pull the plow faster and make up for today's holiday."

A jade is a horse of low quality.

The first countryman said, "I am sure to have my wife as jealous as a turkey, but that's all one. I'll go through with it; let her grumble."

The second countryman said, "Board her as if she were a ship tomorrow night and fill up her empty lower area as if you were filling an empty hold with cargo, and she will forgive you."

The third countryman said, "Yes, all you need to do is to put a fescue in her fist and you shall see her learn a new lesson and be a good lass."

A fescue was a pointer used in teaching. Metaphorically, a fescue was a penis.

The third countryman then asked, "Will we all keep our promise to participate in the Mayday festivities?"

The fourth countryman asked, "What can keep us from doing it?"

The third countryman said, "Arcas will be there."

"And Sennois and Rycas," the second countryman said, "and three better lads never danced under a green tree. And you know which wenches, ha! But will the dainty *domine*, the fastidious schoolmaster, keep his promise, do you think? For he is in charge of everything, you know."

The word "wench" was not necessarily derogatory; it could be used affectionately.

The third countryman said, "He'll eat a hornbook rather than fail. Come on, the matter's too far driven between him and the tanner's daughter to let the matter slip now. The tanner's daughter insists on seeing the Duke, and she insists on dancing, too."

A hornbook is a single sheet of paper covered with and protected by thinly sliced and therefore transparent horn. On the paper are the alphabet, numbers, and the Lord's Prayer.

The fourth countryman asked, "Shall we be merry?"

The second countryman said, "All the boys in Athens can't compete against us. If this were a race, they would be behind us, huffing and puffing and blowing wind against our butts."

He started to dance and said, "And here I'll be and there I'll be, for our town, and here again, and there again. Ha, boys, hurray for the weavers!"

The first countryman said, "This dance of ours must be done in the woods."

The fourth countryman started to object, "Oh, pardon me."

The second countryman confirmed that the dance would be done in the woods during a break in the hunting and along with other rustic celebrations: "By all means. Our thing of learning the schoolmaster says so — in the woods where he himself will edify the Duke most amazingly in our behalves. He's excellent in the woods, but bring him to the plains and his learning makes no cry."

The woods were often hilly and always rustic areas; the plains were level sites where cities could be built. The schoolmaster and the dance supervised by the schoolmaster were suitable for the woods, but not noble enough for the court.

Hunting dogs make a cry when they scent their prey; metaphorically, the schoolmaster's learning would make no cry in the court. It would not be impressive.

The third countryman said, "We'll see the sports, then every man to his tackle."

The tackle was equipment — what was needed for the dance. Performers of a morris dance needed bells.

He added, "And, sweet companions, let's rehearse, by all means, before the ladies see us, and do so sweetly, and God knows what may come of it."

The proverb "To stand to one's tackling" meant "To be ready for anything." The word "stand" also meant "erection." "What may come of it" could be a private activity involving a man and a woman.

The fourth countryman said, "I agree. Once the sports are ended, we'll perform. Let's go, boys, and let's carry on."

Arcite stepped forward and said, "By your leaves, honest friends. Please tell me where you are going."

The fourth countryman asked, "Where we are going? Why, what kind of a question is that?"

Arcite replied, "It is a question to me who doesn't know the answer."

The third countryman answered, "We are going to the games, my friend."

The second countryman asked, "Where were you raised, that you don't know that?"

"I was raised not far from here, sir," Arcite said politely. "Are there such games today?"

The first countryman said, "Yes, indeed, there are, and such as you never saw. Duke Theseus himself will be in person there."

"What pastimes will there be?"

The second countryman said, "Wrestling and running."

He then said to the other countrymen about Arcite, "He is a good-looking fellow."

The third countryman asked, "Will you come along with us?"

"Not yet, sir," Arcite replied.

"Well, sir," the fourth countryman said. "Take your own time."

He then said to the other countrymen, "Come, boys."

The first countryman said quietly to the other countrymen as they were leaving, "I am worried. This fellow has a formidable way of moving his hips that will be of great advantage in wrestling. Look at how his body seems made for wrestling."

The second countryman said quietly, "I'll be hanged, though, if he dares to wrestle. Hang him, the plum porridge! He wrestle? He roast eggs! He's better suited to be an eater than a wrestler! Come, let's go, lads."

The four countrymen exited.

Alone, Arcite said, "This opportunity that I dared not wish for has fallen into my lap. I knew how to wrestle well — the best men called me an excellent wrestler — and I knew how to run swifter than wind ever flew upon a field of corn, furling the abundant ears.

"I'll venture to be there and compete in these sports while I'm in some poor disguise. Who knows whether my brows may not be girt with the garlands of a victor, and who knows whether happiness and good fortune will promote me to a position at court where I may always dwell in sight of the woman I love?"

Alone, the jailor's daughter said, "Why should I love this gentleman? The odds are that he never will love me. I am lowly born, my father is the lowly keeper of his prison, and the man I love is a Prince. To marry him is hopeless; to be his whore is witless and foolish. Damn it! What extremes are we lasses driven to when our fifteenth year has once found us!

"First, I saw him. I, seeing him, thought that he was a handsome man. He has as much to please a woman in him, if he ever chooses to bestow it, as ever these eyes yet looked on.

"Next, I pitied him, and so would any young girl, on my conscience, who ever dreamed, or vowed to give her virginity to a young handsome man.

"Then, I loved him, extremely loved him, infinitely loved him!

"And yet he had a first cousin, as fair as himself, too.

"But Palamon was in my heart, and there, Lord, what a turmoil he causes! To hear him sing in an evening, what a Heaven it is! And yet his songs are sad ones. Fairer spoken was never any other gentleman. When I would come in to bring him water in the morning, first he would bow his noble body, and then he would greet me like this: 'Fair, gentle maiden, good morning. May thy goodness get you a happy husband.' Once he kissed me; I loved my lips all the better for ten days afterward. I wish that he would kiss me every day! He grieves much — and I grieve as much when I see his misery.

"What should I do to make him know I love him? I would like to sexually enjoy him. Let's say I ventured to set him free? What does the law say then?"

Her father the jailer would get in serious trouble if Palamon were to escape from jail.

Snapping her fingers, she said, "Thus much for law or my kindred! I will do it, and this night, or tomorrow, he shall love me."

Theseus, Hippolyta, Pirithous, Emilia, and Arcite talked together. Arcite was in disguise, and he was wearing the garland of a victor. Some attendants and other people were present.

Theseus said to Arcite, "You have done worthily. I have not seen, since Hercules, any man of tougher muscles than you. Whoever you are, you run the best and wrestle the best that these times can boast of."

Arcite replied, "I am proud to please you."

"In what country were you raised?" Theseus asked.

"This country, but far away, Prince Theseus," Arcite answered.

"Are you a gentleman?" Theseus asked.

"My father said so, and he raised me to pursue gentlemanly activities."

"Are you his heir?" Theseus asked.

"I am his youngest son, sir," Arcite replied.

The oldest son was the father's heir.

"Your father, surely, is a happy sire, then," Theseus said, politely assuming that the older son or sons would be as excellent as Arcite.

He then asked, "What accomplishments do you profess to have?"

Arcite replied, "I have a little of all the noble qualities. I knew how to keep a hawk, and I have hallooed well to a deep cry of dogs while hunting. I dare not praise my feats in horsemanship, yet those who knew me would say it was my best accomplishment. Last, and greatest, I would be thought to be a soldier."

"You are perfect," Theseus said. "You have all the accomplishments of a gentleman."

"Upon my soul, he is a handsome man," Pirithous said.

"He is, indeed," Emilia said.

Pirithous said to Hippolyta, "How do you like him, lady?"

Hippolyta replied, "I admire him. I have not seen so young a man be so noble a gentleman, if he has said the truth about his accomplishments."

"Believe him," Emilia said. "His mother was a wondrously beautiful woman. His face, I think, shows that."

"But his body and fiery mind show that he has a brave father," Hippolyta said.

"Notice how his virtue, like a hidden Sun, breaks through his baser garments," Pirithous said.

"He's well begotten, certainly," Hippolyta said. "His father is definitely noble."

Theseus asked Arcite, "What made you seek this place, sir?"

"Noble Theseus," Arcite replied, "I came here to earn fame and do my ablest service to such a well-approved, commendable wonder as your worth, for only in your court, of all the world, dwells fair-eyed Honor."

"All his words are worthy," Pirithous said.

Theseus said to Arcite, "Sir, we are much indebted to you and your travel to and your travail in the games. Nor shall you lose your wish to be in my court."

He then said, "Pirithous, find a place at court for this fair gentleman."

"Thanks, Theseus," Pirithous said.

He then said to Arcite, "Whoever you are, you're my servant, and I shall give you to a most noble service: You will serve this lady, this bright young virgin."

He brought Arcite over to Emilia.

Pirithous then said, "Please treat her goodness with all due respect. You have honored her fair birthday with your virtues, and, as your due, you're hers. Kiss her fair hand, sir."

Arcite replied, "Sir, you're a noble giver."

He then said to Emilia, "Dearest beauty, thus let me seal my vowed faith."

He kissed her hand and added, "When your servant, your most unworthy creature, merely offends you, command him to die, and he shall."

"That would be too cruel," Emilia replied. "If you deserve well, sir, I shall soon see it. You're my attendant, and I'll treat you somewhat better than your rank."

Pirithous said to Arcite, "I'll see you equipped with what you need, and because you say you are a horseman, I must ask you this afternoon to ride — but it is a rough ride."

"I like my horse better that way, Prince," Arcite said. "I shall not then freeze, be motionless, and feel no emotions in my saddle."

Theseus said, "Hippolyta, sweet, you must be ready — and you, Emilia — and you, friend — and all, tomorrow by the sunrise, to celebrate flowery May Day in Diana's wood."

Diana was the Roman goddess of the hunt; she was a virgin goddess.

Theseus said to Arcite, "Serve well, sir, your mistress."

Then he said, "Emily, I hope he shall not go afoot."

Emily said, "That would be a shame, sir, while I have horses."

She then said to Arcite, "Take your choice, and whatever you lack at any time, let me but know it. If you serve me faithfully, I dare assure you that you'll find a loving mistress."

In this culture, the words "servant" and "mistress" had more than one meaning. A mistress could be 1) a female boss or 2) a woman whom a man loved and served. A servant could be 1) an attendant or 2) a lover who served his mistress.

Arcite replied, "If I do not, let me find that which my father always hated: disgrace and blows."

"Go, and lead the way; you have deserved it."

Arcite made a gesture of demurral, but Theseus said, "It shall be so; you shall receive all dues that are fit for the honor you have won. Otherwise, it would be wrong."

He said to Emilia, "Sister-in-law, curse my heart, you have a servant here, who if I were a woman would be my master."

In this culture, "master" sometimes meant "husband."

He added, "But you are wise."

Emilia replied, "I hope that I am too wise for that, sir."

Alone, the jailer's daughter said, "Let all the Dukes and all the Devils roar! Palamon is at liberty. I have risked myself for him, and I have brought him out of prison. I have sent him a mile hence to a little wood where a cedar higher than all the rest spreads like a tall spreading plane tree near a brook, and there he shall stay hidden until I provide him with files and food, for yet his iron bracelets — fetters — are not off.

"Oh, Cupid, god of Love, what a stout-hearted child you are! My father would have preferred to endure cold iron fetters than to do what I have done.

"I love Palamon beyond love and beyond reason or wit or safety. I have made him know it; I have told him. I don't care; I am desperate. If the law should find me and then condemn me for it, some wenches, some honest-hearted maidens, will sing my dirge and tell future times that my death was noble — that I died almost a martyr.

"Whatever path he takes I intend to be my path, too. Surely he cannot be so unmanly as to leave me here. If he does, maidens will not so easily trust men again. And yet he has not thanked me for what I have done; no, he has not so much as kissed me, and that, I think, is not so good; nor could I hardly persuade him to become a free man, he made such scruples of the wrong he did to me and to my father."

Of course, Palamon was reluctant to leave the place where Emilia was near.

The jailer's daughter continued, "Yet I hope, after he reflects more thoroughly, this love of mine will take more root within him. Let him do what he wants with me, as long as he treats me kindly — benevolently and in the way that a man uses a woman — for use me so he shall, or I'll proclaim him, and to his face, no man. I'll tell him that he is impotent.

"I'll right away provide him with necessities and pack my clothes up and wherever there is a path on ground I'll venture, as long as he is with me. Beside him like a shadow I'll forever dwell.

"Within this hour the hubbub will be all over the prison. I will then be kissing the man they are looking for.

"Farewell, father! Get many more such prisoners as Palamon and beget such daughters as myself, and shortly you may keep yourself. You will be in prison and guard yourself, and you will be alone.

"Now I will go to Palamon."

CHAPTER 3

— 3.1 —

The celebration of May Day was in full swing. The noises of hunting and of celebrating were taking place.

Arcite said to himself, "The Duke has been separated from Hippolyta; each took a separate glade. This is a solemn rite they owe bloom-filled May, and the Athenians perform this rite to the fullest.

"Oh, Emilia, Queen of May Day, you are fresher than May, sweeter than her gold buttons — buds — on the boughs, or all the enameled knick-knacks — brightly colored ornaments, aka flowers — of the meadow or garden."

Using the royal plural, he said, "Indeed, we claim also that Emilia is lovelier than the bank of any nymph who makes the stream seem like flowers."

Nymphs are nature spirits who look like young women and who live in or near natural places such as woods and streams. The stream seemed like flowers in May because the stream's surface reflected the flowers growing on its banks.

Arcite continued, "Emilia, you are the jewel of the wood and of the world. Like a nymph, you have blessed a place with your sole presence. I wish that I, poor man whom I am, might occasionally come into your mind and change some cold, chaste thought! It would be a thrice-blessed event to drop into such a mistress' thoughts unexpectedly.

"Tell me, Lady Fortune, you who are my sovereign next after Emily, to what extent I may be proud. I have things to be thankful for. Emily takes strong notice of me, she has made me be near her; and this beauteous morning, the best and most primary of all the year, she presented me with a brace — a pair — of horses. Two such steeds might well be ridden by a pair of Kings in a battlefield where they fought to see who deserved the title to their crowns.

"Alas, alas, poor cousin Palamon, poor prisoner, you so little dream upon my fortune that you think that you yourself are the happier thing because you are so near Emilia. You think that I am at Thebes, and that I am wretched there, although I am free. But if you knew that my mistress breathes on me, and I hear her language, and I live within her eyesight, and sometimes I am so close to her that I can see my reflection in her eyes — oh, cousin, what anger would seize you!"

Palamon, still wearing shackles, emerged from the bush where he had been hiding and shook his fist at Arcite and said, "Traitor kinsman, thou would perceive my anger if these signs of imprisonment — my shackles — were off me, and if this hand of mine owned a sword. By all oaths in one, I and the justice of my love would prove in a trial by combat that thou are a confessed traitor.

"Oh, thou are the most perfidious lord who ever gently looked. You are the lord emptiest of honor who ever bore an honorable coat of arms. You are the falsest cousin whom blood ever made kin!

"Do thou call her thine?

"I'll prove in my shackles, with these hands, which are empty of weapons, that thou lies, and that thou are a very thief in love, a worthless-as-chaff lord, not even worth the name of villain.

"If I had a sword, and if these prison restraints were off me —"

Arcite said politely, " Dear cousin Palamon —"

Palamon replied, "Cozener Arcite, talk to me with language such as is similar to the deeds you have done to me."

A cozener is a cheater, a deceiver.

Arcite said, "Because I do not find inside my breast any gross stuff that makes me anything like what you proclaim me to be, I must continue to use this gentle language I have been using. It is your anger that makes you mistaken about me. Your anger, which is your enemy, cannot be kind to me. Honor and honesty I cherish and depend on, howsoever you fail to see them in me, and with honor and honesty, fair cousin, I'll continue to act and to speak.

"Please state in well-bred terms your griefs, because your argument is with your equal, who professes to prove his course of action innocent with the mind and sword of a true gentleman."

"I wish that you dared, Arcite!" Palamon said.

Arcite replied, "My cousin, my cousin, you have been well informed how much I dare; you've seen me use my sword against the warning of fear. Surely, you would not hear my bravery doubted by another person without you breaking your silence, even if you were in a religious sanctuary."

"Sir, I have seen your actions in such a place that well might justify your manhood," Palamon replied. "You were called a good Knight and a bold

Knight. But the whole week is not fair if it rains any day of the week. Men lose their valiant temper when they lean toward treachery, and then they fight like compelled bears — they would flee if they were not restrained."

In the "sport" of bear-baiting, bears were tied to a stake and then attacked by dogs. The bears could not flee, but were forced to fight.

Arcite said, "Kinsman, you might as well speak this and act it in your mirror as to speak it to the ears of one who now disdains you."

Palamon said, "Come over to me, relieve me of these cold fetters, give me a sword even though it is rusty, and give me the charity of one meal. Come before me then, with a good sword in thy hand, and just say that Emily is thine. If you do these things, I will forgive the trespass thou hast done me — yes, I will. If thou should defeat me in single combat and relieve me of my life, then when brave souls who have died in a manly way seek from me in Hades some news from Earth, they shall get none but this: Thou are brave and noble."

"Calm yourself," Arcite said. "Return to your hawthorn house and hide yourself. With the darkness of the night, I will be here with wholesome food. These fetters of yours I will file off. You shall have garments to wear and perfumes to kill the smell of the prison. Afterward, when you shall stretch yourself and stand up straight and can say, 'Arcite, I am in good shape again,' you shall have your choice of both sword and armor."

"Oh, you Heavens, does anyone so noble dare to engage in such a blameworthy business?" Palamon said. "None but only Arcite. Therefore, none but Arcite in this kind is so bold. Arcite seems to be noble, but he acts ignobly."

Arcite began, "Sweet Palamon —"

Palamon interrupted, "— I embrace you and your offer; I am doing it only for your offer to duel. Sir, without hypocrisy I may not wish more than my sword's edge on your person."

Hunting horns and cornets sounded.

"You hear the horns," Arcite said. "Enter your muset — your hiding place — lest this duel between us be thwarted before we meet."

A muset is literally a hare's lair.

Duke Theseus was an absolute ruler. If he wished to give two people fighting an illegal duel the death penalty, he could. He would definitely thwart the duel.

Arcite continued, "Give me your hand; farewell."

They shook hands.

Arcite then said, "I'll bring you everything you need. Please, take comfort and be strong."

Palamon replied, "Please keep your promise, and do the deed with a frowning brow. Most certainly you do not love and respect me. Be rough with me, and pour this oil — this false courtesy — out of your language. I swear by this air I breathe, I could hit you for each word you speak, if my anger were not restrained by reason."

"Plainly spoken," Arcite said, "yet pardon me for not using hard language. When I spur my horse, I do not chide him; content and anger in me have but one face — they have the same appearance."

The horns sounded.

"Listen, sir," Arcite said, "the horns call the scattered hunters to the banquet; you must guess I have a position there."

"Sir, your attendance there cannot please Heaven, and I know your position is achieved unjustly."

"It is a good title," Arcite said. "I have deserved it. I am persuaded that this argument or lawsuit, which is sick between us, must be cured by bleeding."

Physicians often treated illnesses by bleeding; the bleeding that Arcite meant would be loss of blood in a single combat. Arcite used the word "lawsuit" because quarrels in which someone was accused of treason but the treason could not be proven were settled with a single combat. The two disputants would fight to the death. God was thought to side with the victor, and the victor was in the right and the vanquished was in the wrong.

Arcite added, "I petition you and ask that you will bequeath this quarrel to your sword and talk of it no more."

"Let me say just one word more," Palamon said. "You are going now to gaze upon my mistress, for note well, she is mine —"

"No, then —" Arcite began.

"Please," Palamon said. "You talk of feeding me to breed strength in me. You are going now to look upon a Sun that strengthens what it looks on; there you have an advantage over me, but enjoy it until I may enforce and apply my remedy. Farewell."

The jailor's daughter was alone in the woods. In her hand was a file she had brought for Palamon to use to release himself from his fetters.

She said to herself, "Palamon has misunderstood which thicket I meant, and he has gone wherever his fancy takes him. It is now almost morning. It doesn't matter; I wish it were perpetual night, and darkness were the lord of the world."

A wolf howled.

"Listen, it is a wolf! Grief has slain fear in me, and except for one thing, I care for nothing, and that one thing is Palamon. I don't care if the wolves would bite me as long as he had this file. What if I hallooed for him? I cannot halloo. If I whooped, what would happen then? If he did not answer, I would call a wolf and do him only that service. Either the wolf would find and eat him, or I would save his life by the wolf's finding and eating me.

"I have heard strange howls all this livelong night; why may it not be that the wolves have made prey of him? He has no weapons; he cannot run; the jingling of his fetters might call deadly things to listen, deadly things that have in them a sense to know when a man is unarmed. Deadly things can smell where resistance is possible.

"I'll set it down that he's torn to pieces; many wolves howled together, and then they fed on him; so much for that. Be bold to ring the bell that announces his death.

"How do I stand then? All's done when he is gone. No, no, I lie. My father is to be hanged because of Palamon's escape. I myself will be forced to beg, if I prize life so much as to deny my act of helping Palamon to escape, but that I would not, even if I would try dozens of deaths — die dozens of times in dozens of ways.

"I am bewildered and confused. I have eaten no food for the past two days; I have sipped some water. I have not closed my eyes except when my lids scoured off their brine with tears.

"Alas, dissolve, my life! Let not my sense become unsettled, lest I should drown, or stab, or hang myself.

"Oh, state of nature, fail altogether in me, since your best props are warped! Let me die!

"So, which way now? The best way is the nearest way to a grave. Each step that does not lead me to a grave is torment.

"Look, the moon is down, the crickets chirp, the screech owl and not the rooster announces the dawn.

"All my duties are done except that one I failed at — joining Palamon. But the point is this —"

She hesitated and then said, "An end, which is my death, and that is all."

Arcite, carrying food, wine, and files, arrived in the thicket where he had earlier met Palamon.

He said, "I should be near the place, and then he shouted, "Ho! Cousin Palamon!"

From his hiding place, Palamon asked, "Arcite?"

"The same," Arcite said. "I have brought you food and files. Come forth and fear not; here is no Theseus."

Stepping out of his hiding place, Palamon said, "And here is none as honest as Theseus, Arcite."

"That doesn't matter," Arcite replied. "We'll argue about that later. Come, take courage. You shall not die like a beast. Here, sir, drink — I know you are faint — and then I'll talk further with you."

Palamon said, "Arcite, thou might now poison me."

"I might," Arcite said, "but I must fear you first. Sit down and please, let's have no more of these vain parleys. Let us not, having our ancient reputation for friendship with us, make gossip for fools and cowards."

He raised a bottle of wine and said, "I drink to your health."

"Do!" Palamon said. He needed his health if he were to fight and defeat and kill Arcite.

Arcite drank to show that the wine was not poisoned and then said, "Please sit down, then, and let me entreat you, by all the honesty and honor in you, not to mention this woman we are quarreling over. It will disturb us. We shall have time enough to talk about her."

"Well, sir," Palamon replied. "I'll drink to you."

He drank.

"Drink a good hearty amount; it breeds good blood, man," Arcite said.

A proverb stated, "Good wine makes good blood."

Palamon drank some more, and Arcite asked, "Don't you feel the wine thawing you?"

"Wait," Palamon said. "I'll tell you after a drink or two more."

"Don't drink sparingly," Arcite said. "Duke Theseus has more, cousin. Eat now."

"Yes," Palamon said.

He ate greedily.

"I am glad you have so good an appetite," Arcite said.

"I am gladder that I have so good food for it."

"Is it not mad, strange, bizarre lodging here in the wild woods, cousin?" Arcite asked.

"Yes, for them who have wild consciences," Palamon replied.

"How does your food taste? Your hunger needs no sauce, I see."

A proverb stated, "Hunger is the best sauce."

"Not much," Palamon replied. "But if it did, your sauce is too tart, sweet cousin."

According to Palamon, Arcite was saucy — impudent and flippant.

Palamon held some meat up and asked, "What is this?"

"Venison."

"That's a meat that promotes strength. Give me more wine. Here, Arcite, to the wenches we have known in our days!"

He raised his cup in a toast and said, "The Lord Steward's daughter! Do you remember her?"

"After you, cousin," Arcite replied.

He may have meant that he knew her after Palamon had known her, or he may have meant that Palamon should speak first.

"She loved a black-haired man," Palamon said.

"She did indeed; well, what of it, sir?"

"And I have heard some call him Arcite, and —"

He hesitated.

"Out with it," Arcite said. "Say what you have to say."

Palamon was going to bring up one of Arcite's youthful infatuations, or possibly an early affair, as a way of saying that Arcite was not worthy of loving Emilia.

"She met him in an arbor," Palamon said. "What did she do there, cousin? Play on the virginals?"

Virginals were an early keyboard instrument. The name was often used to make puns on virginity.

"Something she did, sir," Arcite answered.

"What she did made her groan a month for it — or two, or three, or ten."

Possibly, what she did there made her pregnant for nine months and groan in childbirth at the beginning of the tenth month.

Arcite replied — or perhaps counterattacked — by saying, "The Marshal's sister had her share, too, as I remember, cousin, else there are false tales told abroad about her. Will you drink to her?"

"Yes."

Palamon lifted his cup and drank.

"She is a pretty brunette wench," Arcite said.

He hesitated and then added, "There was a time when young men went a-hunting, and a wood, and a broad beech — and thereby hangs a tale."

He sighed.

"For Emily, upon my life!" Palamon said.

Eavesdroppers, if there were any, ought to be forgiven for thinking that Palamon thought that Arcite meant "And thereby hangs a tail for Emily." After all, Arcite had a kind of tail hanging from his crotch, and he and Emily had been a-hunting. But note Palamon's next words.

Palamon added, "Fool, let's stop this strained mirth. I say again that sigh was breathed for Emily. Base cousin, do you dare break our agreement first — our agreement not to speak about Emily?"

"You are wide of the mark," Arcite said. "You have missed the target."

"By Heaven and Earth, there's nothing in thee that is honest."

"Then I'll leave you," Arcite said. "You are a beast now."

"I am what thou make me, traitor," Palamon replied.

Arcite pointed to a package and said, "There's everything you need: files and shirts and perfumes. I'll come again some two hours from now and bring that which shall quiet all."

"A sword and armor," Palamon said.

"Don't fear that I won't bring them," Arcite replied. "You are now too foul. Farewell. Once you get your trinkets — your fetters — off of you, you shall lack for nothing."

"Sirrah —" Palamon began.

The word "Sirrah" was used to address a man of lower social rank than the speaker. The use of the word by Palamon to refer to Arcite, a man of the same social rank, was insulting.

Arcite interrupted, "— I'll hear no more."

He exited.

Palamon said, "If he keeps his promise to return here with weapons and armor, he will die as a result of it."

The jailor's daughter, whose mind was no longer sound, said to herself, "I am very cold, and all the stars are out, too, the little stars and all, that look like spangles or little jewels. The Sun has seen my folly."

She shouted, "Palamon!"

Then, remembering that she thought he was dead, she said, "Alas, no; he's in Heaven.

"Where am I now? Yonder's the sea, and there's a ship. How it tumbles! And there's a rock that lies in hiding under the water. Now, now, the ship beats upon the rock; now, now, now, there's a leak sprung, a sound — a big — one! How they cry!"

She may have been thinking about sex. A "leaky wench" was a woman who had lost her virginity.

She then said, "Open her sails and let her run before the wind, else you'll lose all. Up with a course or two of sail, and tack about and change direction, boys!

"Good night, good night; you're gone.

"I am very hungry.

"I could find a fine frog; he would tell me news from all parts of the world."

She may have possibly thought first of eating the frog and then remembered that animals are often fine helpers in fairy tales.

She continued, "Then would I make a carrack — a large merchant ship — out of a cockleshell, and sail by east and northeast to the King of the pygmies, for he tells fortunes rarely.

"Now my father, twenty to one, will be trussed up in a trice tomorrow morning."

She meant that the odds were twenty to one that her father would be tied up and hanged in the morning. Birds are trussed — their wings and legs are tied to prevent the meat from drying out — before cooking. The word "truss" originally meant a pulley; "in a trice" meant "at a single pull," aka instantly.

She continued, "I'll say never a word."

She then sang this song:

"*For I'll cut my green coat a foot above my knee,*

"And I'll clip my yellow locks an inch below mine [my] eye.

"Hey nonny, nonny, nonny.

"He's [He'll] buy me a white cut [horse, either with a docked tail, or gelded], forth for to ride,

"And I'll go seek him through the world that is so wide.

"Hey nonny, nonny, nonny."

She then said, "Oh, for a prick now, like a nightingale, to put my breast against. I shall sleep like a top else."

Again, she may have been thinking about sex when she said the word "prick." The nightingale was said to press its breast against a thorn in order to stay awake and sing all night. In mythology, the mortal woman Philomela was turned into a nightingale after being raped by her sister's husband, Tereus.

"To sleep like a top" means to sleep soundly. A spinning top is said to "sleep" when it spins in one place and does not move or "walk" from that position.

A schoolmaster and six countrymen were talking; they intended to dance a morris dance for Duke Theseus and other nobles. One of the countrymen was dressed as a Bavian, or baboon.

The schoolmaster said, "Bah, bah, what tediosity and disinsanity is here among you!"

"Tediosity" and "disinsanity" were words of his own coinage.

He continued, "Have my rudiments been labored so long with you, milked unto you, and, by a figure, even the very plum broth and marrow of my understanding laid upon you, and do you still cry 'Where?' and 'How?' and 'Wherefore?'"

By "figure," he meant "figure of speech," something he was fond of. Plum broth and marrow were regarded as tasty foods.

He continued, "You most coarse-frieze capacities, you jean judgments, have I said, 'Thus let be' and 'There let be' and 'Then let be,' and no man understands me?"

"Frieze" was a type of woolen cloth, and "jean" was a type of cotton cloth. Neither was a luxurious cloth, and so the schoolmaster was calling the dancers rough and unsophisticated.

He continued, "*Proh deum, medius fidius!*"

Proh deum is Latin for "Oh, god." *Medius fidius* is Latin for "Help me!"

He continued, "You are all dunces!"

He then went over the plans for the morris dance again:

"Here stand I; here the Duke comes; there are you, nearby in the thicket; the Duke appears; I meet him and to him I utter learned things and many figures; he hears, and nods, and hums in approval, and then cries, 'Rare! Marvelous!' and I go forward. At length I fling my cap up — pay attention to that! Then you do as once did Meleager and the boar — break comely out before him."

The schoolmaster was mistaken about some of the details of Meleager and the boar. Meleager had hunted and killed the boar, which had broken out of a thicket ferociously — not comely, which means "daintily and gently."

He continued, "Like true lovers, cast yourselves in a body — arrange yourselves in a group ready to dance — decently, and sweetly, by a figure, trace and turn, boys."

The "figure" was a dance-figure; by "trace and turn," he meant "dance some steps and revolve."

The first countryman said, "And sweetly we will do it, schoolmaster Gerald."

The second countryman said, "Draw up the company — bring everyone into the proper order. Where's the taborer?"

The third countryman called, "Why, Timothy!"

The taborer arrived. The taborer is a musician who plays on a tabor — a small drum. Often, the taborer plays at the same time a pipe — a wind instrument.

The taborer said, "Here I am, my mad boys. Have at you!"

"Have at you!" announces a coming action. Here the taborer played a few beats on his drum.

The schoolmaster asked, "But I say, where's their women?"

Five women arrived.

The fourth countryman said, "Here's Friz and Maudlin."

"Friz" was perhaps short for Frances, and "Maudlin" was perhaps short for Magdalene.

The second countryman said, "And little Luce with the white legs, and bouncing Barbary."

"Bouncing" meant "vigorous and healthy."

The first countryman added, "And freckled Nell, who never failed her master."

One way to never fail a master is to never say no.

"Where are your ribbons, maidens?" the schoolmaster asked.

The morris dancers sometimes performed while holding streamers.

The schoolmaster continued, "Swim and move gracefully with your bodies, and carry it off sweetly and deliverly, aka nimbly, and now and then make a favor, aka a bow or a curtsey, and make a frisk, aka a caper or jig."

"Don't worry about us," Nell said.

"Where's the rest of the musicians?" the schoolmaster asked.

"Dispersed, as you commanded," the third countryman said. "They are nearby."

"Divide up into couples, then, and let's see what's lacking," the schoolmaster said. "Where's the Bavian, aka baboon?"

Seeing the countryman who would play the baboon, the schoolmaster said, "My friend, carry your tail without offense or scandal to the ladies; don't pretend it is a penis, and be sure you tumble with audacity and manliness, and when you bark, do it with judgment."

In this culture, people thought that baboons were half man and half dog.

"Yes, sir," the countryman who would play the baboon replied.

"*Quo usque tandem?*" the schoolmaster said. "We are lacking a female dancer."

"*Quo usque tandem?*" is the Latin beginning — "How long then?" — of Cicero's first oration against Catiline, who was a danger to the Roman Republic. The speech begins, "*Quo usque tandem abutere, Catilina, patientia nostra?*" It means, "How long then will you, Catiline, abuse our patience?" The schoolmaster was running out of patience.

The fourth countryman said, "We may go whistle; all the fat's in the fire."

"We may go whistle" means "We won't get what we want, so we may as well leave and whistle." "To go whistle" is an idiom for "have no chance of success."

"The fat is in the fire" is an idiom for "Bad consequences will follow." When fat falls into fire, the result is a burst of flames. Here it also means, figuratively, "Our work was done in vain." The fat is often tasty, and if the fat falls into the fire, one can't eat it.

The schoolmaster said, "We have, as learned authors utter, washed a tile; we have been *fatuus* — foolish — and labored vainly."

"To wash a tile" is a proverb that means "Our work was done in vain." Tiles are used to line fireplaces. Each time a fire is lit, the tiles get dirty.

The second countryman said about the missing female dancer, "This is that scornful piece, that scurvy hilding — that good-for-nothing — who gave her promise faithfully she would be here. I am talking about Cicely, the tailor's daughter.

"The next gloves that I give her shall be made of cheap dogskin, if she fails me once more — you can tell everyone, Arcas, that she swore by wine and bread, aka the Eucharist, she would not break her promise."

The schoolmaster said, "An eel and a woman, a learned poet says, unless by the tail and with your teeth you hold, will both fail."

It is difficult to hold a live wet eel by the tail. The schoolmaster's language brings to mind the image of holding a woman's "tail" by one's teeth. A proverb stated, "Who has a woman has an eel by the tail."

He continued, "In manners, this was false position."

He meant that this breach of etiquette was analogous to a false premise in logic.

The first countryman said, "May a fire-ill infect her!"

In this culture, "fire" was a slang word for "vagina." In other words, the first countryman was saying, "May she suffer from a diseased vagina, aka suffer from a venereal disease."

The first countryman continued, "Does she flinch now?"

The idiom "My ears are burning" means "I think someone is talking about me." If Cicely, the tailor's daughter, could hear what the first countryman was saying about her, she would flinch.

"What shall we determine to do, sir?" the third countryman asked.

"Nothing," the schoolmaster said. "Our business is become a nullity, yes, and a woeful and a piteous nullity."

A nullity is a no-event, a nothing.

The fourth countryman said, "Now, when the credit of our town lay on it, now to be moody and disagreeable, now to piss on the nettle!"

Nettles sting. Being careless while pissing on nettles could very well make someone moody and disagreeable.

The fourth countryman continued, "Go thy ways; get out of town! I'll remember thee. I'll fix thee!"

The jailor's daughter, now mentally ill, walked over to the group. She sang this song:

"*The* George Alow *[name of a ship] came from the south,*

"*From the coast of Barbary-a,*

"*And there he met with brave gallants [sailors] of war,*

"*By one, by two, by three-a.*

"*'Well hailed, well hailed, you jolly gallants,*

"*And whither now are you bound-a?*

"*'Oh, let me have your company*

64

"'Till I come to the sound-a.'"

She said, "There was three fools, who fell out and argued about an owlet," and then she sang this song:

"The one he said it was an owl,

"The other he said nay,

"The third he said it was a hawk,

"And her bells were cut away."

In this culture, falconers tied small bells to the feet of hawks and falcons.

The third countryman said, "There's a dainty madwoman, master, who comes in the nick of time, as mad as a March hare."

The obsolete word "nick" means "the critical moment."

Hares are mad in March because that is the mating season.

The third countryman continued, "If we can get her to dance, we are all right again. I promise that she'll do the most marvelous gambols."

"A madwoman?" the first countryman said. "We are made, boys."

To be "made" is to be "assured of success."

The schoolmaster said to the jailor's daughter, "And are you mad, good woman?"

She replied, "I would be sorry else. Give me your hand."

"Why?"

"So I can tell your fortune."

She looked at his hand and said, "You are a fool. Count to ten.

"I have posed for him a task he cannot do. Buzz!"

One way of testing for mental competence is to have someone count to ten on his or her fingers.

She continued, "Friend, you must eat no white bread; if you do, your teeth will bleed extremely."

Two more modern meanings of "to bleed white" are 1) to drain of resources, slowly or completely, and 2) to shed colorless, unhealthy blood ("to bleed white" used hyperbolically). And if someone's gums were diseased, red blood would be readily apparent on white bread.

In this culture, a folk belief was that a man's teeth ached and bled when his wife was pregnant.

She continued, "Shall we dance? I know you; you're a tinker. Sirrah tinker, stop no more holes but what you should."

One way to stop a hole is to fill it with a penis.

The schoolmaster said, "*Dii boni!*"

The Latin words mean, "Good gods!"

He then asked, "A tinker, damsel?"

"Or a conjurer," the jailer's daughter said. "Raise me a Devil now, and let him play '*Chi Passa*' on the bells and bones."

"Raise me a Devil" can mean "Erect a penis for me." Boccacio wrote a story (Third Day, Tenth Story) in his *Decameron* about putting the Devil in Hell. In the story, of course, Hell was a vagina, and the Devil was a penis.

"*Chi Passa Questa Strada*" is Italian for "Who Passes Through This Street." It is a dance tune.

Bones were used to make percussion music.

The schoolmaster said to the second countryman, "Go, take her, and fluently persuade her to a peace."

The schoolmaster wanted the second countryman to calm the jailer's daughter so she could dance.

The schoolmaster continued, "*Et opus exegi, quod nec Iovis ira, nec ignis.*"

The Latin words of this incomplete sentence mean, "And I have completed a work of literature that neither Jove's anger nor fire."

These Latin words were from the end of Ovid's *Metamorphoses*, except Ovid wrote "*Iamque*" instead of "*Et.*" This is the complete sentence: "*Iamque opus exegi, quod nec Iovis ira nec ignis nec poterit ferrum nec edax abolere vetustas.*" In this sentence Ovid boasted that his fame would continue as a result of this literary masterpiece. The Latin words mean, "And I have now completed a work of literature that neither Jove's anger nor fire nor steel nor time will destroy." Jove is Jupiter, the King of the gods.

The schoolmaster continued, "Strike up the music, and lead her in to the dance."

The second countryman said, "Come, lass, let's trip it. Let's dance."

"I'll lead," the jailer's daughter said.

"Do, do!" the second countryman said.

"You have done it persuasively, and cunningly," the schoolmaster said to the second countryman.

Horns sounded. Theseus and the other nobles were coming this way. There was no time for the jailer's daughter to rehearse.

The schoolmaster said, "Away, boys! I hear the horns. Give me some room for solitary meditation, and listen for your cue."

All but the schoolmaster hid themselves.

The schoolmaster said to himself, "Pallas Athena, inspire me!"

At the beginning of many epic poems, the epic poet asks a deity or deities for inspiration.

Theseus, Pirithous, Hippolyta, Emilia, and a train of others arrived.

Theseus said, "The stag went this way."

"Stay, and edify!" the schoolmaster said.

By "edify," the schoolmaster meant "be instructed."

"What have we here?" Theseus asked.

"Some country entertainment, upon my life, sir," Pirithous answered.

"Well, sir, go forward," Theseus said to the schoolmaster. "Go ahead. We will 'edify.'"

Attendants brought out a chair and some stools.

Theseus said, "Ladies, sit down. We'll stay for the entertainment."

Theseus, Hippolyta, and Emilia sat.

The schoolmaster said, "Thou doughty Duke, all hail! All hail, sweet ladies!"

Punning on the word "hail," Theseus said quietly, "This is a cold beginning."

The schoolmaster had referred to Theseus with the informal "thou," which was taking a liberty, but May Day was a holiday and Theseus was normally a benevolent ruler, and so he let it pass.

The schoolmaster said, "If you but [show us] favor, our country pastime made is.

"We are a few of those collected here

"That ruder tongues distinguish [call] 'villager.'

"And to say verity, and not to fable,

"We are a merry rout, or else a rabble,

"Or company, or by a figure, chorus,

"That before thy dignity will dance a morris.

"And I that am the rectifier [director] of all,

"By title *pedagogus* [educator], that let fall

"The birch upon the breeches of the small ones,

"And humble with a ferula [cane, using for beating an unruly student] the tall ones,

"Do here present this machine [show], or this frame [framework].

"And, dainty Duke, whose doughty [brave and persistent] dismal fame"

The schoolmaster meant by "doughty dismal fame" that Theseus' fame was terrible and frightening to his enemies.

"From Dis to Daedalus, from post to pillar,"

Dis was the god of Hades, which Theseus had once visited and from which he had returned alive. Daedalus had constructed the labyrinth on Crete to house the half-man, half-bull monster called the Minotaur. Theseus had killed the Minotaur.

"Is blown abroad, help me, thy poor well-willer,

"And with thy twinkling eyes look right and straight

"Upon this mighty 'Morr,' of mickle [great] weight [importance] —

"'Is' now comes in, which being glued together

"Makes 'Morris,' and the cause [reason] that we came hither."

The schoolmaster had displayed two placards. On one was written "Morr"; on the other was written "is." Brought together, they spelled "Morris."

"The body of our sport, of no small study,

"I first appear, though rude, and raw, and muddy,

"To speak before thy noble grace this tenner [tenor, aka content],

"At whose great feet I offer up my penner [case for carrying pens]."

Now he began to list the characters the dancers would be portraying:

"The next, the Lord of May and Lady bright,

"The Chambermaid and Servingman by night

"That seek out silent hanging;"

The chambermaid and servingman would seek at night an alcove behind a hanging that would hide their amorous activity.

"then mine Host

"And his fat Spouse, that welcomes to their cost

"The galled traveler, and with a beckoning

"Informs the tapster to inflame the reckoning;"

The host of the inn and his fat wife would invite the traveler to have a drink on the house, but the host would signal to the tapster to add the drink to the traveler's bill.

"Then the beest-eating Clown;"

"Beest" is the milk that a cow gives immediately after giving birth. Some people regard beest as undrinkable, and other people use it in porridges.

"and next the Fool,

"The Bavian [baboon] with long tail and eke [also] long tool [penis],

"*Cum multis aliis* [Latin for "and all the others"] that make a dance;

"Say 'ay,' and all shall presently advance."

Theseus said, "Ay, ay, by all means, dear *Domine*."

Domine is Latin for "schoolmaster."

Pirithous said, "*Produce*! Lead them forward!"

"*Produce*" is Latin for "Lead forward."

The schoolmaster said, "*Intrate, filii.* Come forth and foot it. Dance."

"*Intrate, filii*" is Latin for "Come in, boys!"

Music played. The countrymen, countrywomen, and jailer's daughter performed a morris dance.

The schoolmaster then made this speech:

"Ladies, if we have been merry

"And have pleased ye with a derry,

"And a derry and a down,

"Say the schoolmaster's no clown.

"Duke, if we have pleased thee too

"And have done as good boys should do,

"Give us but a tree or twain [two]

"For a Maypole, and again,

"Ere [Before] another year run out,

"We'll make thee laugh, and all this rout."

Theseus said to the schoolmaster, "Take twenty, *Domine*."

He then asked Hippolyta, "How are you, my sweetheart?"

She replied, "I have never been so pleased, sir."

Emilia said, "It was an excellent dance, and as for the prefacing speech by the schoolmaster, I have never heard a better."

Theseus said, "Schoolmaster, I thank you. One of you see to it that they are all rewarded."

An attendant gave the schoolmaster money.

Pirithous also gave the schoolmaster money, saying, "And here's something to paint your pole with."

The pole was a May pole, but the schoolmaster could possibly use his share of the money to treat his sweetheart and get a part of his body wet.

Theseus said, "Now let's return to our sports again. We have a stag to hunt."

The schoolmaster made this speech:

"May the stag thou hunts stand long [and withstand the dogs],

"And thy dogs be swift and strong;

"May they kill him [the stag] without lets [hindrances],

"And the ladies eat his dowsets."

"Dowsets" were the stag's testicles; they were considered a delicacy.

The horns sounded, and Theseus, Hippolyta, Emilia, Pirithous, and the train of attendants exited.

The schoolmaster said to the dancers, "Come, we are all made."

The dance had been successful, and Theseus and Pirithous had tipped well.

The schoolmaster continued, *Dii deaeque omnes*, you have danced marvelously, wenches."

"*Dii deaeque omnes*" is Latin for "All you gods and goddesses."

Palamon emerged from the bush where he had been hiding.

He said to himself, "My cousin gave his word to visit me again about this hour, and to bring with him two swords and some pieces of good armor for us to wear. If he should fail to show up, he's neither a man nor a soldier. When he left me, I did not think a week could have restored my lost strength to me because I was grown so low and crestfallen with my lack of food and shelter. I thank thee, Arcite, thou are still a fair foe, and I feel myself, with this refreshing, able once again to endure danger. To delay our duel any longer would make the world think, when it heard about it, that I ate as if I were being fattened like a swine for the market and not as if I were a soldier preparing for a fight. Therefore, this blessed morning shall be the last before our duel, and whatever sword he refuses after I offer him the first choice of swords, if it but holds true and does not break, that is the sword I will kill him with. It is justice. So, may love and good fortune be for me!"

Arcite kept his word. He arrived now, carrying pieces of armor and two swords.

"Oh, good morning," Palamon said.

"Good morning, noble kinsman," Arcite replied.

"I have put you to too much effort, sir," Palamon said.

"That too much, fair cousin, is only a debt owed to honor and my duty."

"I wish that you were so honorable in all aspects of your life, sir," Palamon said. "I could wish you were as kind a kinsman as you force me to find that you are a beneficial foe so that my embraces, and not my blows, might thank you."

"I shall think either — blows or embraces — well done, a noble recompense," Arcite said.

"Then I shall pay you your recompense," Palamon said.

Arcite said, "Defy me in these fair terms, and you appear more than a mistress to me. No more anger, as you love anything that's honorable! We were not bred to talk, man; when we are armed and both of us are upon our guards, then let our fury, like the meeting of two tides, fly strongly from us, and then to whom the birthright of this beauty truly pertains, by which I mean to whom Emilia belongs as a birthright — without upbraidings, scorns, despisings of our persons, and such poutings, which are fitter for girls and schoolboys — will be seen, and quickly. We will find out whether Emilia is yours or mine.

"Will it please you to arm, sir? Or if you feel yourself not ready yet and not yet furnished with your old strength, I'll wait, cousin, and every day I will talk you back into health during my spare time away from my official duties. I am friends with you, and I could wish I had not said that I loved Emilia even though keeping my love secret would have killed me. But I must not flee from loving such a lady and from justifying my love for her in single combat."

"Arcite, thou are so brave an enemy that no man but thy cousin is fit to kill thee. I am well and vigorous. Choose your arms."

"You choose, sir," Arcite said.

"Will thou exceed and outdo me in every respect, including good manners, or are thou doing it to make me spare thee?"

"If you think so, cousin, you are deceived, for as I am a soldier, I will not spare you."

"That's well said," Palamon said.

"You'll find that what I said is true," Arcite said.

"Then, as I am an honest man and love with all the justice of affection, I'll pay you fully the punishment you deserve," Palamon said. "I will have justice and love on my side."

Palamon choose a piece of armor: "I'll take this."

Arcite said: "This other piece is mine, then."

He then said, "I'll arm you first."

"Do," Palamon replied.

Arcite began to put the piece of armor on him.

Palamon said, "Please tell me, cousin, where did thou get this good armor?"

"It is Duke Theseus," Arcite answered, "and to say the truth, I stole it."

He then asked whether the armor was pinching Palamon: "Do I pinch you?"

"No."

"Isn't it too heavy?"

"I have worn lighter armor," Palamon answered, "but I shall make it serve."

"I'll buckle it tightly," Arcite said.

"By all means."

"Do you care for a grand guard?" Arcite asked.

This was a joke. A grand guard is a heavy piece of armor used in jousting and when fighting on horseback. Arcite and Palamon had no horses, and Arcite was unable to carry two grand guards in addition to everything else he was carrying.

"No, no, we'll use no horses," Palamon said. "I perceive that you would like to fight on horseback."

"I am indifferent," Arcite said. "It doesn't matter to me either way."

"Truly, so am I," Palamon said. "Good cousin, thrust the buckle through far enough."

"I assure you that I will," Arcite said.

"My helmet is next."

Normally, the next piece of armor would be for the arms.

Arcite asked, "Will you fight bare-armed?"

"If we do, we shall be all the nimbler because of it."

"But use your gauntlets, though," Arcite said.

Palamon picked up a pair, but Arcite said, "Those are of lesser quality. Please take mine, good cousin."

"Thank you, Arcite. How do I look? Has my flesh fallen much away? Have I lost a lot of weight?"

"Truly, very little," Arcite said. "Love has used you kindly."

This was an insult. The conventional idea of a lover at the time was of someone who lost much weight because he was so much in love that he did not eat.

Deliberately no longer using the respectful "you," Palamon said, "I'll promise thee that I'll strike home. I'll hit my target, which is thee."

"Do, and don't spare me," Arcite said. "I'll give you cause not to spare me, sweet cousin."

"Now it's your turn, sir," Palamon said.

He began to arm Arcite and said, "I think that this armor's very like the armor, Arcite, that thou wore that day the three Kings fell, but lighter."

"That was a very good suit of armor, and on that day, I well remember that you outdid me, cousin. I never saw such valor. When you charged upon the left wing of the enemy, I spurred my horse hard to catch up to you, and under me I had a very good horse."

"You did, indeed," Palamon said. "You had a bright bay horse, I remember."

"Yes, but all my labor was in vain. You outstripped me, nor could my wishes reach you. Yet I accomplished a little by imitating you."

"Your accomplishments came about more through manly virtue and courage," Palamon said. "You are modest, cousin."

"When I saw you charge first, I thought I heard a dreadful clap of thunder break from the troop."

"But always before that thunder flew the lightning of your valor," Palamon said. "Wait a little while. Isn't this piece too tight?"

"No, no, it is fine," Arcite replied.

"I would have nothing hurt thee but my sword," Palamon said. "For you to suffer a bruise from my making your armor too tight would be dishonorable to me."

"Now I am perfectly armed," Arcite said.

"Draw back, then."

"Take my sword," Arcite said. "I regard it as the better sword."

"I thank you, but no," Palamon said. "Keep it; your life depends on it. Here's the other sword; if it doesn't break, I ask no more for all my future hopes. A sword that doesn't break is all that I need to achieve my hopes for the future. May my cause and honor guard me!"

"And may my love guard me!" Arcite said.

They bowed in several directions, and then they stood and faced each other.

They were pretending that their illegal private duel was a formal, officially sanctioned trial by combat. In a trial by combat, a crowd of spectators and officials would be present and would be bowed to.

Arcite asked, "Is there anything else you have to say?"

"This only, and then no more," Palamon replied. "Thou are my aunt's son and so that blood we desire to shed is mutual — thine blood is in me, and my blood is in thee. My sword is in my hand, and if thou should kill me, then the gods and I forgive thee. If there is a place prepared for those who sleep in honor after death, I wish the weary soul belonging to the one of us who falls and dies will win it. Fight bravely, cousin. Give me thy noble hand."

Arcite said, "Here, Palamon."

As they shook hands, Arcite added, "This hand shall never again come near thee with such friendship."

"I commend — honor — thee," Palamon said.

"If I fall, curse me, and say I was a coward," Arcite said, "for only cowards dare to die in these just trials. Once more I say farewell, my cousin."

"Farewell, Arcite."

They began to fight, but hunting horns sounded and they stopped.

Arcite said, "Listen, cousin, listen, our folly has ruined us!"

"In what way?"

"The Duke is hunting, as I told you," Arcite said. "If we are found dueling, we are wretched. Oh, retire, for honor's sake, and for your own safety, immediately go into your bush again. Sir, we shall find too many hours to die in. Gentle cousin, if you are seen, you will perish instantly for breaking out of prison, and I, if you reveal to Theseus who I am, will perish instantly because of the contempt I showed for Theseus by not obeying his command to leave this country and never return. Then all the world will scorn us, and say we had a noble quarrel between us, but we had a base way of resolving that quarrel."

"No, no, cousin," Palamon said. "I will no more be hidden, nor put off this great adventure to a second trial. I know your cunning, and I know your cause."

Palamon believed that Arcite did not want to fight because he knew that he was in the wrong.

He continued, "He who faints now, may shame take him! Put thyself upon thy immediate guard —"

Theseus or no Theseus, Palamon wanted to fight to the finish. Either he or Arcite must die.

"You must be mad," Arcite said.

"If thou don't put thyself upon thy immediate guard, I will make the advantage of this hour my own. I fear less what shall come to threaten me than I fear my fortune."

Palamon did not fear Theseus; he did fear that his fortune might be to lose Emilia.

He added, "Know, weak cousin, I love Emilia, and in that I'll bury thee and everything else that crosses and attempts to thwart my love."

"Then let come what can come," Arcite said. "Thou shalt know, Palamon, I dare as well to die as to talk or to sleep. Only this frightens me: The law will have the honor of our ends."

The ends were their deaths, which would be dishonorable because they would be found guilty of fighting an illegal duel. The law would receive honor, however, because Palamon and Arcite would be sentenced to death in accordance with the law, which would be justly and honorably enforced.

Arcite said, "Have at thy life!"

This meant, "Prepare to be attacked!"

Palamon replied, "Look well after your own life, Arcite."

They began to fight again.

Hunting horns sounded. Theseus, Hippolyta, Emilia, Pirithous, and a train of attendants arrived.

Immediately aware that an illegal duel was taking place, Theseus said, "What ignorant and mad malicious traitors are you, who against the tenor and content of my laws are making battle thus, like Knights appointed, without my permission and without officers of arms?"

He swore, "By Castor, son of Jove, both of you shall die."

Palamon said, "Keep thy word, Theseus.

"We are certainly both traitors; both of us are despisers of thee and of thy goodness. I am Palamon, who cannot love thee. I broke out of thy prison. Think well what that deserves.

"And this is Arcite. A bolder traitor never trod thy ground, a falser person never seemed to be a friend. This is the man whom Pirithous begged mercy for. Arcite was banished from your Kingdom. This is a man who shows contempt for thee and whatever thou dare to do. And in this disguise, against thine own edict and command, he pursues thy sister-in-law, that benevolent bright star, that bringer of good fortune, the fair Emilia, whose servant — if there exists a right in seeing first and in first bequeathing one's soul to — justly I am, and which is more, he dares think that Emilia is his.

"Like the most trusty lover that I am, I called him now to answer for this treachery. If thou are as thou are reputed to be, great and virtuous and the true judge of all injuries, say, 'Fight again,' and thou shall see me, Theseus, do such a just act that thou thyself will envy it. Then thou can take my life; I'll encourage thee to do it."

"Oh, Heaven," Pirithous said. "What more than man is this!"

"I have sworn an oath that both of you shall die," Theseus replied.

Arcite said, "We aren't seeking thy words of mercy, Theseus. It is to me a thing as soon and easy to die as for thou to say it, and I will be no more moved than thou will be.

"Whereas this man calls me traitor, let me say thus much: If being in love is treason, in service of so excellent a beauty, then since I love most, and in that fidelity to that love will perish, since I have brought my life here to confirm it, since I have served her truest, worthiest, since I dare kill this cousin who denies it, so let me be most traitor, and you will please me when you sentence me to death.

"As for scorning thy edict of banishment, Duke, ask that lady why she is beautiful, and why her eyes command me to stay here and love her; and if she says that I am a traitor, then I am a villain fit to lie unburied."

Palamon said, "You shall have pity on us both, Theseus, if to neither of us you show mercy. Close, as you are just, your noble ears against us. As you are valiant, for your cousin Hercules' soul, whose twelve strong labors crown his memory, let Arcite and I die together at the same instant, Duke, only let him fall just a little before I do, so that I may tell my soul he shall not have Emilia."

Theseus said, "I grant your wish, for to say the truth, your cousin has offended me ten times more than you, for I gave him more mercy than you found, sir, although your offenses were no more than his."

He then ordered, "Let no one here speak for them, for before the Sun sets, both shall sleep forever."

"It's a pity," Hippolyta said. "Now or never, sister, speak in such a way that you will not be denied; otherwise, that face of yours will bear the curses of future ages because of the deaths of these cousins."

"In my face, dear sister, I find no anger toward them, nor no ruin," Emilia said. "The misadventure of their own eyes kills them. Yet to show that I am a woman and have pity, my knees shall grow to the ground unless I get mercy for these two men."

She knelt.

She then said, "Help me, dear sister; in a deed so virtuous, the powers of all women will be with us."

Hippolyta knelt.

As they spoke, their words followed close upon each other's.

Emilia said, "Most royal brother —"

Hippolyta said, "Sir, by our tie of marriage —"

Emilia said, "By your own spotless honor —"

Hippolyta said, "By that faith, that fair hand, and that honest heart you gave me —"

Emilia said, "By that which you would invoke to cause pity in another, by your own virtues infinite —"

Hippolyta said, "By valor, by all the chaste nights I have ever pleased you —"

The chaste nights in which Hippolyta pleased Theseus were the nights in which they engaged in chaste, aka moral, sex — the sex of a married couple.

Theseus said, "These are strange, solemn appeals."

"I'll join in, too," Pirithous said.

He knelt and said, "By all our friendship, sir, by all our dangers, by all you love most: wars and this sweet lady —"

Emilia said, "By that which you would have trembled to deny a blushing maiden —"

According to the protocol of chivalry, a Knight was obliged to help a maiden in distress.

Hippolyta said, "By your own eyes; by strength, in which you swore I went beyond all women, and almost all men, and yet I yielded, Theseus —"

Pirithous said, "To crown all this, by your most noble soul, which cannot hold back the giving of deserved mercy, I beg first —"

Hippolyta said, "Next hear my prayers —"

Emilia said, "Last let me entreat, sir —"

Pirithous said, "For mercy."

Hippolyta said, "Mercy."

Emilia said, "Mercy on these two Princes."

Theseus said to all the petitioners, "You make my faith reel. I swore that they would die, but you make me waver."

He said to Emilia, "Say that I felt compassion on both of them, how would you say that I should show it to them?"

Emilia, Hippolyta, and Pirithous rose from their knees.

Emilia said, "You should have mercy upon their lives, but with their banishments. Let them live, but in exile."

"You are a true — typical — woman, sister-in-law," Theseus said. "You have pity, but you lack the understanding of where and how to use it. If you desire to save their lives, invent a way safer than banishment. Can these two live, and have the agony of love about them, and not kill one another? Every day they would fight about you; hourly they would fight in public with their swords and they would publicly bring your honor in question.

"Be wise, then, and here forget them; it concerns your reputation and my oath equally. I have said they will die. It's better that they fall by the law than by fighting one another. Don't cause my honor to bow. Let my honor stand tall by my keeping my oath."

"Oh, my noble brother-in-law," Emilia said, "that oath was rashly made when you were angry. Your reason when you are not angry will not allow you to keep it. If such vows stand for fixed, final, irreversible will, all the world must perish. Besides, I have another oath against yours, an oath you made to me of more authority and I am sure of more love than this rash oath. The oath you made me was not made in passion, either, but in good heed and with careful consideration."

"What oath is that, sister-in-law?" Theseus asked.

"Urge it home, brave lady," Pirithous said. "Be persuasive."

Emilia said, "You swore to me that you would never deny me anything that was fit for my modest petitioning and your free granting.

"I tie you to your word now; if you fail in it, think how you maim your honor — for now that I am set a-begging, sir, I am deaf to everything but your compassion. Think of how the loss of these two men's lives might breed the ruin of my name. Gossip!

"Shall anything that loves me perish because of me? That would be a cruel wisdom. Do men prune the straight young boughs that blush with a thousand blossoms because they may be rotten?

"Oh, Duke Theseus, the excellent mothers who have groaned in childbirth for these two men, and all the longing maidens who ever loved, if your vow to have these two men killed stands, shall curse me and my beauty, and in their funeral songs for these two cousins, they will despise my cruelty, and cry for woe to fall upon me, until I am nothing but the scorn of women.

"For Heaven's sake, save their lives, and banish them."

"On what conditions?" Theseus asked.

"Make them swear that they never again will fight over me, or even say that they know me. Make them swear never again to tread upon your Dukedom, and to be, wherever they shall travel, always strangers to one another."

Palamon said, "I'll be cut to pieces before I take this oath! Forget I love her? Oh, all you gods, despise me then! I don't dislike your sentence of banishment, as long as we may fairly carry our swords and our argument with us; if we can't do that, then don't trifle with us, but instead take our lives, Duke. I must love, and will love, and for that love must kill and dare to kill this cousin on any piece of ground the Earth has."

"Will you, Arcite, accept these conditions in order to save your life?" Theseus asked.

"He's a villain, if he does," Palamon said.

"These are real men!" Pirithous said.

"No, never, Duke Theseus," Arcite replied. "It would be worse to me than begging to save my life in such a base manner. Even though I think I never shall enjoy Emilia, yet I'll preserve the honor of affection, and die for her — no matter how horrible a death I suffer and even if you make death a Devil!"

Theseus said, "What may be done? For now I feel compassion."

"Let your compassion not fall again, sir," Pirithous said.

"Tell me, Emilia," Theseus said, "if one of those two men were dead, as one must be, are you content — satisfied and without complaint — to take the other to be your husband? They cannot both enjoy you. They are Princes as excellent as your own eyes, and as noble as fame yet ever spoke of. Look upon them, and, if you can love one of them, end this quarrel. Choose to marry one, and the other will die. I give my consent to this."

He then asked Palamon and Arcite, "Are you content, too, Princes?"

Palamon and Arcite replied, "With all our souls."

"The man whom Emilia refuses to marry must die then," Theseus said.

"He will die any death you can invent, Duke," Palamon and Arcite replied.

Palamon said, "If I fall and die because of words that come from that mouth, I fall and die with favor, and lovers yet unborn shall bless my ashes."

Arcite said, "If she refuses to marry me, yet my grave will wed me, and soldiers will sing my epitaph."

Theseus said to Emilia, "Make your choice of whom to marry, then."

"I cannot, sir," Emilia said. "They are both too excellent. A hair shall never fall from these two men on my account."

"What will become of them?" Hippolyta asked.

"This is what I command," Theseus said, "and, by my honor, once again, what I command will stand, or both shall die: You shall both return to your country, and each of you within this month, accompanied by three fair Knights, will appear again in this place, in which I'll plant a pillar, and whichever of you, before us who are here, can force his cousin by fair and Knightly strength to touch the pillar, that victorious man shall enjoy Emilia. The other will lose his head, as will all his three friends who accompanied him. He will accept and not begrudge his fall and death, and he will not think that he dies with interest in this lady.

"Will this content you two?"

"Yes," Palamon replied.

He added, "Here, cousin Arcite, I am friends again with you until that hour."

He held out his hand.

They shook hands.

Arcite said, "I embrace you."

They hugged.

Theseus asked, "Are you content, sister-in-law?"

"Yes, I must be content, sir," Emilia replied, "or else both will die."

Theseus said to Palamon and Arcite, "Come, shake hands again, then, and take heed, as you are gentlemen, that this quarrel will sleep until the hour I have named, and hold your course. Be sure not to fight until you have returned with your Knights."

"We dare not fail thee, Theseus," Palamon said.

Palamon and Arcite shook hands again.

"Come, I'll give you now treatment that is fitting for Princes and friends," Theseus said. "When you return, whoever wins I'll settle here in Athens. Whoever loses, I'll be sure to weep upon his bier."

CHAPTER 4

— 4.1 —

The jailer and a friend talked together.

The jailor said, "Have you heard anything more? Was anything said about me concerning the escape of Palamon? Good sir, remember!"

The friend replied, "I heard nothing because I came home before the business was fully ended. Yet I did perceive, before I departed, a great likelihood of both the two Princes being pardoned because Hippolyta and fair-eyed Emily, upon their knees, begged with such proper pity that the Duke, I thought, stood wavering whether he should follow his rash oath or the sweet compassion of those two ladies. And, to support them, that truly noble Prince, Pirithous — half of Theseus' own heart — set in, too, so that I hope all shall be well. I never heard one question about your name or his escape."

"I pray to Heaven that continues to be the case," the jailor said.

Another of the jailor's friends arrived.

The second friend said, "Be of good comfort, man; I bring you news — good news."

Good news is welcome," the jailer replied.

"Palamon has cleared you in his escape and has gotten a pardon for you, and he has revealed how and by whose means he escaped, which was your daughter's, whose pardon has been procured, too, and the prisoner, Palamon, not to be held ungrateful to her goodness, has given a sum of money toward her marriage — a large one, I assure you."

"You are a good man and always bring good news," the jailer said.

The first friend asked, "How did everything end?"

"Why, as it should have ended," the second friend said. "They who never begged without prevailing had their petitions fairly granted; the prisoners have their lives."

"I knew it would be so," the first friend said.

"But there are new conditions, which you'll hear of at a better time," the second friend said.

"I hope they are good," the jailer said.

"They are honorable," the second friend said. "How good they'll prove to be I don't know."

"We will find out," the first friend said.

The wooer of the jailer's daughter arrived and asked the jailer, "Alas, sir, where's your daughter?"

"Why do you ask?" the jailer asked.

"Oh, sir, when did you last see her?" the wooer asked.

The second friend whispered to the first friend, "Look at the expression on the wooer's face!"

"This morning," the jailer said.

"Was she well? Was she in health? Sir, when did she sleep?" the wooer asked.

The first friend whispered to the second friend, "These are strange questions."

The jailer said, "I do not think she was very well, for now you make me remember her, and on this very day I asked her questions and she answered me much unlike her usual self. She answered me very childishly, very sillily, as if she were a fool, as innocent as a young child or a simpleton, and I was very angry. But what of her, sir?"

"She has nothing but my pity," the wooer said. "But you must know why, and it is as good that you learn the reason from me as from another who loves her less."

"Well, sir?" the jailer said.

"No, sir, not well," the wooer said.

"Is she not right in the head?" the first friend asked.

"Is she not well?" the second friend asked.

"It is too true," the wooer said. "She is mad."

"It cannot be," the first friend said.

"Believe that you'll find it's true," the wooer said.

"I half suspected what you told me," the jailer said. "May the gods comfort her! Either this is on account of her love for Palamon, or fear of my suffering bad consequences because of his escape, or both."

"It is likely," the wooer said.

"But why all this haste in coming to me, sir?" the jailer asked.

"I'll tell you quickly," the wooer said. "As I recently was fishing in the great lake that lies behind the palace, from the far shore — which is thickly set with reeds and sedges — as I was patiently attending to my fishing pole, I heard a voice, a shrill one, and I listened attentively. I clearly heard that someone was singing, and by the smallness of the voice I knew it had to be a boy or a woman. I then left my fishing pole unattended, came near to where the voice was coming from, but did not yet perceive who made the sound because the rushes and the reeds had so enclosed it. I lay down and listened to the words she sang, for then, through a small glade cut by the fishermen, I saw that the singer was your daughter."

"Please go on, sir," the jailer said.

The wooer continued, "She sang much, but the song had no sense. I only heard her repeat this often: 'Palamon is gone, is gone to the wood to gather mulberries; I'll find him tomorrow.'"

The first friend said, "Pretty soul!"

The wooer continued, "She also said, 'His shackles will betray him; he'll be captured, and what shall I do then? I'll bring a bevy of girls, a hundred black-eyed maidens who love as I do, with garlands of daffodils on their heads, with cherry lips and cheeks of damask roses, and we'll all dance an antic, aka grotesque dance, before the Duke, and beg his pardon.'

"Then she talked of you, sir. She said that you must lose your head tomorrow morning, and she must gather flowers to bury you, and see the house made tidy. Then she sang nothing but '*Willow, willow, willow*,' and in between stanzas she said, 'Palamon, fair Palamon,' and 'Palamon was a brave young man.'

"The place was knee-deep in rushes where she sat. A wreath of bulrushes crowned her careless locks of hair, and on her were fastened a thousand fresh water-flowers of several colors, so that I thought she looked like the fair nymph who feeds the lake with waters, or like the messenger goddess Iris, who is also the goddess of the rainbow, newly dropped down from Heaven.

"She made rings out of rushes that grew nearby, and to them spoke the prettiest posies: '*Thus our true love's tied*,' '*This you may lose or loose [untie], not me*,' and many other ones."

Poesies are brief romantic sayings engraved on the inside of gold and silver rings.

The wooer continued, "And then she wept, and sang again, and sighed, and with the same breath smiled and kissed her hand."

The second friend said, "Alas, what a pity it is!"

"I made my way to her," the wooer said, "She saw me and immediately jumped into the water. I saved her and set her safely on land, and immediately she slipped away, and to the city she went with such a cry and swiftness that, believe me, she left me far behind her. Three or four people I saw from far off encounter her — one of them I knew to be your brother — whereupon she stopped and fell, and with difficulty was taken away."

She may have been exhausted or may not have wanted to accompany her uncle and his companions.

The wooer continued, "I left them with her and came here to tell you."

The jailer's brother, the jailer's daughter, and others arrived.

The wooer said, "Here they are now."

The jailor's daughter sang, "*May you never more enjoy the light.*"

She then asked, "Isn't this a fine song?"

"Oh, a very fine one," the jailor's brother replied.

"I can sing twenty more," the jailor's daughter said.

"I think you can," the jailor's brother said.

"Yes, truly can I," the jailor's daughter said. "I can sing 'The Broom' and 'Bonny Robin.' Aren't you a tailor?"

"Yes," the jailor's brother said.

"Where's my wedding gown?" the jailor's daughter asked.

"I'll bring it tomorrow," the jailor's brother said.

"Do so very early," the jailor's daughter said. "Otherwise I must go out of my home to summon the maidens and pay the minstrels, for I must lose my maidenhead by cocklight — the time just before the cock crows to announce the dawn. It will never thrive otherwise."

She sang, "*Oh, fair. Oh, sweet.*"

The jailer's brother said to the jailer, "You must indeed endure this patiently."

"That is true," the jailer said.

"Good evening, good men," the jailer's daughter said. "Please tell me, did you ever hear of one young Palamon?"

"Yes, girl, we know him," the jailer replied.

"Isn't he a fine young gentleman?"

"He is, love," the jailer answered.

The jailer's brother whispered to the others, "By no means contradict her; if you do, she will then be troubled far worse than she is now."

The first friend said to the jailer's daughter, "Yes, he's a fine man."

"Oh, is he so?" the jailer's daughter said, suddenly suspicious. "You have a sister."

"Yes, I do," the first friend said.

"But she shall never have him — tell her that — because of a trick that I know," the jailer's daughter said. "You'd best look after her, for if she sees him once, she's gone — she's pregnant. She's done and undone — seduced and ruined — in an hour. All the young maidens of our town are in love with him, but I laugh at them and let them all alone. Isn't this a wise course of action?"

"Yes," the first friend said.

"There are at least two hundred now with child by him — there must be four; yet I keep close for all this, close as a clam."

"Close as a clam" is an idiom for "safe from harm." When a clam's shell is closed, it is safe from harm.

The jailer's daughter continued, "And all these must be boys — he has the knack for having only boys — and at ten years old they must all be gelded so they can be musicians and sing about the wars of Theseus."

"This is strange," the second friend said.

"As strange as you ever heard, but say nothing," the jailer's daughter said.

"No," the first friend said.

The jailer's daughter said, "They come from all parts of the Dukedom to him. I'll promise you, he had last night not so few as twenty to dispatch — to take care of and then send away. He'll tickle it up in two hours, if his hand be in."

"To tickle it" means "to bring to a happy ending" and "to tickle up" means "to arouse." "If his hand be in" means "if he is in good form."

The jailer said quietly, "She's lost past all cure."

The jailer's brother said quietly, "Heaven forbid, man!"

The jailer's daughter said to her father, "Come here. You are a wise man."

The first friend asked quietly, "Does she recognize him?"

The second friend said quietly, "No. I wish she did."

The jailer's daughter asked her father, "Are you the master of a ship?"

"Yes," he said, humoring his daughter.

"Where's your compass?"

"Here," the jailer said, pretending he had a compass.

"Set it to the north," the jailer's daughter said. "And now direct your course to the wood, where Palamon lies longing for me. As for the tackling, you can rely on me."

She said to the others, "Come, weigh anchor, my hearts, and do it cheerily."

Everyone pretended to be raising an anchor and sailing a ship to humor her:

"Owgh, owgh, owgh!" These are grunting sounds made when doing hard work such as weighing an anchor — raising it when ready to depart.

"The anchor is up!"

"The wind's fair!"

"Top the bowline!" This means to tighten the rope that steadies a sail's edge.

"Out with the main sail! Where's your whistle, master?"

The jailer's brother said, "Let's get her in!"

"Up to the top, boy!" the jailer said. This means to climb to the top of the mast.

"Where's the pilot?" the jailer's brother said.

"Here," the first friend said.

"What can you see?" the jailer's daughter asked.

"A fair wood," the second friend said.

"Bear for it, master. Steer for it," the jailer's daughter said. "Tack about! Turn the ship's head into the wind!"

She sang, "*When Cynthia with her borrowed light.*"

Cynthia was the goddess of the Moon, whose light is borrowed because it reflects the light of the Sun.

Emilia stood alone, holding two miniature pictures. One picture depicted Palamon; the other picture depicted Arcite.

She said, "I could still bandage those wounds up that must otherwise open and bleed to death for my sake."

She meant that she could heal the wounded friendship between Palamon and Arcite so that other, physical wounds would not open.

She continued, "I'll choose one of them, and by so doing end their strife. Two such young handsome men shall never fall and die because of me; their weeping mothers, following the dead cold ashes of their sons, shall never curse my cruelty."

Emilia looked at one of the pictures.

She then said, "Good Heaven, what a sweet face Arcite has! If wise Nature, with all her best endowments, all those beauties she sows into the births of noble bodies, were here a mortal woman, and had in her the shy, modest denials of young maidens, yet without a doubt she would run mad for this man.

"What an eye, of what a fiery sparkle and lively sweetness this young prince has! Here in Arcite's eye, Cupid, the god of Love, himself sits smiling. With just such another smile, frolicsome Ganymede set Jove afire, and he forced the King of the gods to snatch him — the good-looking boy — up and set the boy by him, Jove; the boy became a shining constellation."

Ganymede was a beautiful human boy whom Jupiter, aka Jove, King of the gods, kidnapped and made his cupbearer. Later, Ganymede was transformed into the constellation Aquarius.

Emilia continued, "What a forehead of what a spacious majesty he exhibits, arched like the great-eyed Juno's but far sweeter — smoother than Pelops' shoulder!"

Juno, wife of Jupiter, had large eyes.

Pelops' shoulder was made of ivory. His father, Tantalus, killed him, cooked him, and served him to the gods. One goddess, Demeter, ate some of his shoulder before the trickery was discovered. The gods brought Pelops back to life and sentenced his father, Tantalus, to everlasting punishment in the Land of the Dead. He stands in a stream of water with fruit-bearing branches above his head. Whenever he stoops to drink, the water level lowers and the stream dries up. Whenever he reaches for fruit to eat, the wind blows the branches just out of his reach. He is forever thirsty and hungry, and water and fruit are always just out of his possession.

Emilia continued, "Fame and Honor, I think, from Arcite's brow as from a promontory that ends in a point in Heaven, should clap their wings and sing to all the world under Heaven the loves and fights of gods and men such as are like them."

Emilia looked at the other picture.

She then said, "Palamon is only a foil to Arcite."

A foil is a setting for a jewel. The foil is of much lesser value than the jewel and serves to show off the jewel's luster.

Emilia continued, "Compared to Arcite, Palamon is only a dull shadow. He's swarthy and thin, of an eye as heavy and sorrowful as if he had lost his mother. He has a lethargic temperament. There is no liveliness in him, no alacrity. Of all this sprightly sharpness there is not a smile — he has no trace of Arcite's keenness of spirit.

"Yet these things that we regard as errors and flaws may become him. Narcissus was a sad but Heavenly boy."

Narcissus was beautiful, and he fell in love with his reflection in a stream.

Emily continued, "Oh, who can find the reasoning of woman's love? I am a fool; my reason is lost in me. I have no ability to choose, and I have lied so vilely that women ought to beat me.

"On my knees I ask you for your pardon, Palamon. You and only you are beautiful, and these are the eyes — these are the bright lamps of beauty — that command and threaten love, and what young maiden dares to oppose them?

"What a bold gravity, and yet inviting, this brown manly face has! Oh, Love, from this hour this is the only complexion for me."

She put aside Arcite's picture and said, "Lie there, Arcite."

She then said, "You, Arcite, are a changeling compared to Palamon; you are a mere gypsy, and this is the noble body."

Fairies were said to exchange ugly babies for beautiful babies.

She continued, "I am besotted and utterly lost. My virgin's constancy has fled from me. For if my brother-in-law had but just now asked me which of the two men I loved, I would have run mad for Arcite. Now, if my sister would ask me, I would run even madder for Palamon.

"Let both pictures stand side by side. Now, come ask me which man I prefer, brother-in-law. Alas, I don't know! Ask me now, sweet sister. I may as well go and look because I have no answer!

"What a mere child is Fancy, who, having two fair toys of equal sweetness, cannot choose between them, but must cry for both."

A gentleman entered the room.

"What is it, sir?" Emilia asked.

"Madam, I bring you news from the noble Duke, your brother-in-law," the gentleman said. "The Knights have come."

"To end the quarrel?" Emilia asked.

"Yes."

"I wish I might end — die — first!" she said. "What sins have I committed, Diana, goddess of chastity, that my unstained youth must now be soiled with the blood of Princes, and my chastity be made the altar where the lives of lovers — two greater and two better men never yet gave mothers joy — must be the sacrifice to my unhappy beauty?"

Theseus, Hippolyta, Pirithous, and some attendants entered the room.

Theseus said to an attendant, "Bring them in quickly, by all means. I long to see them."

He said to Emilia, "Your two contending lovers have returned, and with them their fair Knights. Now, my fair sister-in-law, you must love one of them."

"I would rather love both, so that neither for my sake should fall and die prematurely."

"Who saw them?" Theseus asked.

"I saw them for a short time," Pirithous said.

"And I did, too," the gentleman said.

A messenger entered the room.

"From whence have you come, sir?" Theseus asked.

"From the Knights."

"Please tell us, you who have seen them, what kind of men they are."

"I will, sir," the messenger said, "and I will say what I truly think. Six braver spirits than these Knights Arcite and Palamon have brought, if we judge by their outside appearance, I have never seen nor read of.

"The Knight who stands in the first place with Arcite, by his appearance, should be a valiant man. Judging by his face, he is a Prince — his very looks say that he is one. His complexion is nearer a brown than black — stern and yet noble — which shows that he is hardy, fearless, and pleased by dangers. The circles of his eyes show fire within him, and he looks like an angry lion. His hair hangs long behind him, black and shining like ravens' wings; his shoulders are broad and strong. His arms are long and muscular, and on his thigh a sword hangs by a finely made baldric, aka leather shoulder strap. He uses his sword to put his seal on business when he frowns. A better sword, I swear by my conscience, was never a soldier's friend."

"You have described him well," Theseus said.

"Yet he is a great deal short, I think, of the Knight who's the first with Palamon," Pirithous said.

"Please tell us about him, friend," Theseus said.

"I guess he is a Prince, too," Pirithous said, "and, if it may be, greater than a Prince, for his appearance has all the trappings of honor in it. He's somewhat bigger than the Knight the messenger spoke of, but he has a face far sweeter; his complexion is, like a ripe grape, ruddy. He has felt without doubt what he fights for — love — and so he is readier to make this cause his own. In his face appears all the fair hopes of what he undertakes, and when he's angry, then a steady valor, not tainted with extremes, runs through his body and guides his arm to accomplish brave things. He cannot feel fear; he shows no such soft temper. His hair's yellow-blonde — tightly curled, thickly twined like ivy bushes, and this Knight is not to be destroyed by thunder and lightning."

The Knight looked like a victor, and people in this culture believed that the wreath of a victor protected him from lightning. People in this culture also believed that some plants, including ivy, were impervious to thunder and lightning.

Pirithous continued, "In his face the uniform of the warlike maiden goddess Athena appears; his face is pure red and white, for as of yet no beard has blessed him. And in his rolling eyes sits Victory, as if she always meant to crown his valor. His nose stands high, a characteristic of honor. His red lips, after fights, are fit for ladies."

"Must these men die, too?" Emilia asked.

The others ignored her question.

Pirithous continued, "When he speaks, his words sound like a trumpet. All the parts of his body are as a man would wish them, strong and well built. He carries a well-steeled axe; the handle is made of gold. His age is approximately twenty-five."

The messenger said, "There's another — a little man, but of a tough soul. His appearance seems to be as great as any. Fairer promises in such a body I have never yet looked on."

"Oh, is he the one who's freckle-faced?" Pirithous asked.

"The same, my lord," the messenger said. "Are they not charming freckles?"

"Yes, they are," Pirithous said.

"I think," the messenger said, "being so few, and well distributed, they show great and fine art in nature. He's blonde, white-haired — not a dyed wanton white, but such a manly color that is next to an auburn. He is tough and agile, which shows he has an active soul. His arms are brawny, lined with strong muscles — to the shoulder-piece gently they swell, like newly pregnant women, which shows that he is prone to work hard, never fainting under the weight of arms. He is always valiant-hearted, even when at rest, but when he stirs and moves, he is a tiger. He's grey-eyed, which shows that he yields compassion where he conquers. He is sharp at spying advantages, and where he finds them, he's swift to make them his. He does no wrongs, nor does he endure wrongs from others. He's round-faced, and when he smiles he shows that he is a lover; when he frowns, he shows that he is a soldier. About his head he wears the winner's oak — the crown of oak leaves given to a victorious soldier — and in it is stuck the favor of his lady."

Ladies would give favors — scarfs or gloves — that Knights would display conspicuously to show which lady they were fighting for.

The messenger continued, "His age is approximately thirty-six. In his hand he holds a jousting-lance embossed with silver."

"Are they all like this?" Theseus asked.

"All of them are the sons of honor," Pirithous answered.

"Now, as I have a soul, I long to see them," Theseus said.

He then said to Hippolyta, who as an Amazon knew about women fighting, "Lady, you shall see men fight now."

"I wish to see it," Hippolyta said, "but not fighting for this cause, my lord. They would show themselves bravely if they were fighting about the titles of two Kingdoms. It is a pity that love should be so tyrannous."

She said to Emilia, who was crying, "Oh, my soft-hearted sister, what do you think? Don't weep tears until their wounds weep blood. Woman, this duel must happen."

Theseus said to Emilia, "You have steeled and given them strength with your beauty."

He said to Pirithous, "Honored friend, to you I give the management of the field of honor; please prepare it and make it suitable for the persons who must use it."

"Yes, sir," Pirithous replied.

"Come, I'll go and visit them," Theseus said. "I cannot wait until they appear — the reports I have just heard about them have set me on fire to see them now. Good friend, be royal; be like a King when it comes to making the field of honor magnificent."

"No splendor shall be lacking," Pirithous said.

Everybody but Emilia exited.

She said to herself, "Poor wench, go and weep, because whoever wins will lose a noble cousin on account of your sins."

Emilia's "sins" were her beauty and her virtues that had caused both Arcite and Palamon to fall in love with her to the extent that they wanted to kill each other so that the survivor could marry her and have her.

The jailer, the wooer of the jailer's daughter, and a doctor talked together.

The doctor said, "Her insanity is more evident at some phases of the moon than at other phases, isn't it?"

The jailer replied, "She is continually in a derangement that causes no harm to others. She sleeps little, lacks altogether her appetite, except that she often drinks, dreams of another and a better world, and whatever broken piece of matter — that is, whatever nonsense — she's about, the name 'Palamon' lards it, so that she stuffs every topic with his name and fits it to every question. She stuffs the name 'Palamon' into her conversation as if she were stuffing bacon into lean meat to flavor it."

The jailer's daughter arrived.

The jailer said, "Look, here she comes. You shall see her behavior for yourself."

They stood to the side and watched her.

The jailer's daughter said, "I have quite forgotten the song. The chorus of it was '*down-a, down-a*,' and it was penned by no worse man than Geraldo, Emilia's schoolmaster."

She probably meant the foolish and pretentious Gerald, who was not Emilia's schoolmaster.

The jailer's daughter continued, "He's as full of wild fancies, too, as any man who may walk upon his legs, for in the next world Dido will see Palamon, and then she will be out of love with Aeneas."

Apparently, Gerald had written, or the jailer's daughter thought he had written, a song about Palamon, Dido, and Aeneas. In Vergil's *Aeneid*, Dido, the Queen of Carthage, committed suicide after Aeneas deserted her after a love affair in order to go to Italy and fulfill his fate of becoming an important ancestor of the Romans. Aeneas visited the Land of the Dead and saw Dido, but she would not speak to him.

The doctor whispered to the jailer and the wooer of the jailer's daughter, "What nonsense is this? Poor soul."

"This is the way she is all day long," the jailer said.

The jailer's daughter said, "Now for this charm that I told you about, you must bring a piece of silver on the tip of your tongue, or else there will be no ferry."

The ancient Romans put a coin on the tongue of a corpse so that the dead person's soul could pay the ferryman Charon to ferry the soul across a river to the Land of the Dead.

The jailer's daughter continued, "Then if it is your opportunity to come where the blessed spirits are, there's a sight now! We maidens who have our hearts broken, cracked to pieces with love, we shall come there, and do nothing all day long but pick flowers with Proserpine."

Proserpine, whose Greek name was Persephone, was picking flowers when Pluto, god of the Land of the Dead, kidnapped her, took her to the Underworld, and made her Queen of the Land of the Dead.

The jailer's daughter continued, "Then I will make Palamon a nosegay — a bouquet of flowers. Then let him pay attention to me. And then —."

"How prettily and charmingly she's out of her senses!" the doctor said. "Let's watch her a little further."

"Indeed, I'll tell you, sometimes we go to barley-break, we of the blessed," the jailer's daughter said.

Barley-break was a game played by couples. In the middle was an area called Hell, and the other couples would try to run through Hell without being caught. If they were caught, they became catchers.

The jailer's daughter continued, "Alas, it is a sore life they have in the other place, in Hell — such burning, frying, boiling, hissing, howling, chattering, cursing — oh, they have a harsh measure, so take heed! They don't get measure for measure; they get more than a measure for their punishment.

"If one should be mad, or if one should hang or drown themselves, thither they go, Jupiter bless us, and there shall we be put in a cauldron of lead and usurers' grease, amongst a whole million of cutpurses, and there boil like a lower side of bacon that will never be cooked enough."

Usurers' grease was the sweat of usurers.

"How her brain creates fantasies!" the doctor said.

The jailer's daughter continued, "Lords and courtiers who have made maidens pregnant are in this place. They shall stand in fire up to the navel and in ice up to the heart, and there the offending part burns and the deceiving part freezes."

In this culture, "stand" was slang for "erection," and "fire" was slang for "vagina."

The jailer's daughter continued, "Truly, it is a very grievous punishment, so one would think, for such a trifle. Believe me, one would marry a leprous witch to be rid of such a punishment, I'll assure you."

In some cultures, a man's punishment can be waived if a woman agrees to marry him. These seducers in Hell, however, did not marry the maidens they made pregnant.

The doctor said, "How she keeps up this fancy! It is not an engrafted madness, but a very thick and profound melancholy."

The doctor meant that her illness was not firmly implanted insanity, but that she was instead seriously melancholic.

The jailer's daughter said, "To hear there a proud lady and a proud city wife howl together — I would be a beast and I'd call it good entertainment."

The proud lady would be of a much higher social rank than the city lady and would be mortified to be punished with her.

The jailer's daughter continued, "One cries, 'Oh, this smoke!' The other cries, 'Oh, this fire!' One cries, 'Oh, that I ever did it behind the arras!' and then howls. The other curses a persistently wooing fellow and her garden house."

One of the women had had illegitimate sex in an alcove behind a wall hanging — an arras. The other had had illegitimate sex in the garden house.

The jailer's daughter sang, "*I will be true, my stars, my fate.*"

She then exited.

"What do you think of her, sir?" the jailer said.

"I think she has a perturbed mind, which I cannot minister to," the doctor said.

"Alas, what then can we do?" the jailer asked.

"To your knowledge, did she ever love any man before she beheld Palamon?"

The jailer said, "I had once, sir, great hopes that she had fixed her liking on this gentleman, who is my friend."

The wooer said, "I did think so, too, and I would think I had made a great bargain if I could give half my wealth so that both she and I, at this present moment, stood unfeignedly and genuinely on the same terms. I would give half my wealth to make her sane again."

The doctor realized that the jailer's daughter was ill because of unrequited love — an illness that could definitely be treated. Her illness was a deep melancholy that could be cured with the help of the wooer.

The doctor said, "That intemperate surfeit of her eyes has distempered her other senses. They may return and settle again to execute their preordained faculties, but they are now in a most extravagant vagary."

This society believed that love entered one's body through the eyes. The jailer's daughter's love-sickness for Palamon had disordered her other senses, but they could be made to perform their proper function instead of being disordered.

The doctor said to the jailer, "This is what you must do. Confine her to a place where the light may seem to steal in rather than be permitted. A dark room is good for patients like her."

He then said to the wooer, "Take upon you, young sir, her friend, the name of Palamon; pretend to be him, and say that you have come to eat with her, and to talk of love. This will catch her attention, for this is what her mind beats upon and wholly concerns itself with; other objects that are inserted between her mind and eyes become the tricks and vagaries of her madness. Sing to her such youthful songs of love as she says Palamon has sung in prison. Come to her adorned with as sweet flowers as the season is mistress of, and to them make an addition of some other compounded perfumes that are grateful to the senses.

"All these things shall be suitable for Palamon because Palamon can sing, and Palamon is sweet and every good thing. Desire to eat with her, serve food to her, drink to her, and constantly every now and then intermingle your plea for her grace and your acceptance into her favor.

"Learn what maidens have been her companions and playmates, and let them come to her with the name 'Palamon' in their mouths, and appear with love-tokens, as if they were wooing her on his behalf."

The doctor said to the jailer, "She is living in a falsehood, and it must be combated with other falsehoods. She believes in a false reality, and we will lie to her to bring her back to the real world. This may bring her to eat, to sleep, and to reduce what's now out of square in her into its former regulated and normal state."

Tricking a mentally ill patient into eating and sleeping often helped the patient.

The doctor continued, "I have seen this work how many times I don't know, but I have great hope to make the number one more by doing this. I will between the passages of this project come in with my own remedies. Let us put this plan into execution and hasten the outcome, which we should not doubt will be good."

CHAPTER 5

— 5.1 —

Theseus, Pirithous, Hippolyta, and some attendants were present in an area in which three altars were set up. Each of the three altars was dedicated to a god: Mars, god of war; Venus, goddess of love; and Diana, goddess of chastity.

Theseus said, "Now let them enter and before the gods offer their holy prayers. Let the temples burn bright with sacred fires, and the altars in hallowed clouds present their billowing incense to those above us. Let nothing due to the gods be lacking. Those who have a noble work in hand will honor the very gods who love them."

"Sir, they are entering," Pirithous said.

Cornets sounded. Palamon and Arcite and their Knights entered.

Theseus said, "You valiant and strong-hearted enemies, you royal related foes, who this day come to blow out that nearness that flames between you, set aside your anger for an hour and, dove-like and peaceably, before the holy altars of your helpers, the feared-by-all gods, bow down your stubborn bodies. Your ire is more than mortal; so may your help be. And because the gods are watching you, fight with justice. I'll leave you to your prayers, and between you I part my wishes. I wish both of you good fortune."

"May honor crown the worthiest!" Pirithous said.

Theseus, Pirithous, and Theseus' train of attendants exited.

Palamon said to Arcite, "The sands of the hourglass are running now, and by the time the last grain falls one of us will be dead. Think only this: Think that if there were anything in me that strove to appear my enemy in this business, were it one eye against another, one arm oppressed by my other arm, I would destroy the offender, cousin — I would although it were a part of myself. Then from this gather how I should regard you."

Palamon intended to kill Arcite.

Arcite replied, "I am working to push your name, your long-established friendship, and our biological relationship out of my memory, and in the selfsame place to seat something I would destroy. So hoist we the sails that these vessels must bring to port even where the Heavenly Limiter pleases."

Arcite intended to kill Palamon.

The Heavenly Limiter is God, Who sets a limit to the extent of our lives.

"You speak well," Palamon said. "Before I turn and leave, let me embrace you, cousin."

They embraced.

Palamon then said, "This I shall never do again."

"This is one farewell," Arcite said. "It is our last farewell."

"Why, let it be so. Farewell, cousin," Palamon said.

"Farewell, sir," Arcite said.

Palamon and his Knights exited.

Arcite said, "Knights, kinsmen, lovers, yes, my sacrifices who are risking your lives for me, true worshippers of Mars, whose spirit expels the seeds of fear and the apprehension that is always the father of fear, go with me before the altar of the god of our profession.

"At Mars' altar, ask him to give you the hearts of lions and the endurance of tigers, yes, the fierceness, too, and yes, the speed, also — to press ahead, I mean; otherwise, we would wish to be snails if we were to retreat.

"You know my prize must be won with bloodshed; strength and great deeds must put a triumphal garland on my head. The garland placed on my head will be made of the Queen of flowers — roses, which are associated with virgins such as Emilia. Our prayer, then, must be to Mars, who makes the battlefield a cistern brimful with the blood of men. Give me your aid, and bend your spirits towards him."

They went to Mars' altar, fell on their faces before it, and then knelt.

Mortals' relationships with the gods can be personal, familiar relationships, and so when praying mortals can use "thou" and "thee" to refer to the gods.

Arcite prayed, "Thou mighty one, who with thy power has turned the green of the ocean to the red color of blood, whose approach the omens of comets prewarn and prophesy, whose havoc proclaims a vast number of unburied skulls in the battlefield, whose breath blows down the teeming harvest of Ceres, the Roman goddess of grain, who plucks with your powerful hand mason-built turrets from blue clouds of smoke, who both makes and breaks the stony girths of cities, I ask that you this day furnish me, your pupil, the youngest follower of your military drum, with military skill, so that to advance your praise I may advance my streamer, and because of you be styled the lord of the day. Give me, great Mars, some sign of your pleasure."

Here they fell on their faces as they had done formerly, and they heard the clanging of armor, with a short burst of thunder, like the burst of a battle, whereupon they all rose and bowed to the altar.

Arcite continued his prayer: "Oh, great corrector of disorderly, abnormal times, shaker of over-ripe, rotten states, you grand decider of dusty and old titles, who heals with blood-letting the Earth when it is sick, and cures the world of the excess of people, I take your signs auspiciously, and in your name I march boldly to my goal.

"I believe that this sign tells me that I will get what I want: victory in this battle."

He then said to his Knights, "Let's go."

Arcite and his Knights exited.

Palamon and his Knights entered, and Palamon said, "Our stars must glisten with new fire, or be today extinct. Either we are victorious in battle, or we die today. Our subject of contention is love, which if the goddess of love grants, she gives victory, too. So then blend your spirits with mine, you Knights whose lavish nobleness makes my cause your personal hazard. You are risking your lives to help me gain the woman I love. To the goddess Venus, we commit our proceeding and we implore her to use her power on our side in the battle."

Palamon and his Knights went to Venus' altar, fell on their faces before it, and then knelt.

Palamon prayed, "Hail, sovereign Queen of secrets, who has the power to call the fiercest tyrant from his rage and weep in front of a girl because he loves her. You have the might even with an eye-glance to choke Mars' drum and turn the battle alarm into whispers — you can quiet threats of war and turn them into whispers. You can make a cripple wave his crutch, and cure him even before Apollo, god of healing, can cure him. You can force the King to be his subject's vassal, and induce stale old men to dance. The bald bachelor, who, like frivolous boys jumping over small bonfires, skipped over your flame of love in his youth, you can catch at age seventy and make him, to the mockery of his hoarse throat, abuse youthful love songs by singing them.

"What godlike power do you not have power over? To Phoebus Apollo, you added flames hotter than his; the Heavenly fires scorched his mortal son, and your flames scorched him."

Palamon was referring to Phoebus Apollo's mortal son Phaëthon. Jove's Heavenly fire — the thunderbolt — had scorched Phaëthon, and Venus' Heavenly fire — the fire of love — had scorched Phoebus Apollo.

Venus, as the goddess of love, was able to make Apollo feel the fire of love and fall in love with either goddesses or mortal women. Her son Cupid, the god of love, could do the same thing. Cupid looks like a young boy, and he has a bow and arrows. Apollo made fun of him for being a boy who played with a man's weapons, so Cupid shot him with an arrow that made him fall in love with the mortal woman Daphne.

Palamon continued, "You can also make the huntress, Diana, goddess of chastity and of the moist Moon, fall in love and throw her bow away and sigh."

The Moon is said to be moist because it controls the tides.

Venus made Diana fall in love with the shepherd boy Endymion.

Palamon continued, "Take to your grace me, your vowed soldier, who bears your yoke of love as if it were a wreath of roses, and yet your yoke is heavier than lead itself and stings more than nettles. You have made me fall in love with Emilia.

"I have never been foul-mouthed against your law. I have never revealed love secrets, for I knew none — and I would not reveal them, even if I had known all the love secrets that existed. I have never tried to seduce any man's wife, nor would I ever read the libelous attacks against women that were written by licentious wits. I never at great feasts have sought to reveal the indiscretions of a beauty, but instead I have blushed at the simpering, affected, smirking sirs who did. I have been harsh to those who boasted about sexual sins, and I have hotly asked them if they had mothers — I had a mother, who was a woman, and these boasters were wronging women.

"I knew a man who was eighty years old — this I told them to show that I understood your power — who made a bride of a lass of fourteen; you have and had the power to put life into dust. The aged rheumatism had twisted his once-healthy foot into an unnatural position, the gout had knit his fingers into knots, and torturing convulsions had almost pulled his globular, protruding eyes from their sockets. The result was that what was life in him seemed to be torture. This man made of skin and bones had by his young and beautiful wife a boy, and I believed it was his, for she swore it was, and who would not believe her?

"In brief, I am to those who prate and have done what they said they did, no companion. I am to those who boast and have not done what they said they did, a defier. I am to those who want to commit sexual sins but cannot, a rejoicer — I rejoice in their impotence. Truly, I do not respect a man who tells about secret intrigues in the foulest way, and I do not respect a man who reveals sexual secrets with the boldest language.

"Such a one I am as I have said I am, and I vow that no lover has ever yet made a sigh truer than I.

"Oh, then, most soft sweet goddess, give me the victory of this battle, which is true love's merit, and bless me with a sign of your great pleasure."

Music played, and doves fluttered. Palamon and his Knights fell again upon their faces, and then on their knees.

Palamon prayed, "Oh, you who reign from within the mortal bosoms of those from age eleven to age ninety, whose hunting ground is this world and whose game is we herds of humans, I give you thanks for this fair token, which being laid to my innocent true heart, arms in assurance my body to this business. I believe that this sign tells me that I will get what I want: Emilia."

He then said to his Knights, "Let us rise and bow before the goddess."

They rose and bowed.

Palamon said, "The time for the battle is coming on."

They exited.

The soft music of recorders played. Emilia and some of her female attendants arrived. She was wearing white, and her hair was loose about her shoulders. On her head she wore a wreath made of wheat stalks. A female attendant wearing white held up the train of Emilia's dress; the female attendant's hair was decorated with flowers. Another female attendant in front of Emilia was carrying a figure of a deer made of silver. On the deer's back was a place where incense and sweet perfumes could be burned. Her attendants stood to the side, and Emilia put the figure of the silver deer upon the altar of Diana and set fire to the incense and sweet perfumes as a sacrifice. Emilia and her attendants then curtsied and knelt.

Emilia said, "Oh sacred, shadowy, chaste, and constant Queen, abandoner of revels, mute contemplative, sweet, solitary, you are as white as you are chaste, and you are as pure as is the wind-fanned snow. To your female Knights you allow no more blood — sexual passion — than will make a blush, which is their order's robe. I, your female priest, am humble here before your altar. Oh, deign to look on your virgin follower — me — with your rare green eye, which never yet beheld anything spotted and impure. And, sacred silver mistress, lend your ears — which never hear scurrilous words, and into whose ports wanton sounds have never entered — to my petition, which is seasoned with holy fear.

"This is the last of my vestal office; I will no longer serve you as a maiden. I am bride-habited but maiden-hearted; although I am wearing the clothing of a bride, I still have the heart of a maiden. A husband will be given to me, but I don't know who will be my husband.

"Out of two men who wish to marry me, I should choose one, and pray for his success, but I am not guilty of selecting one. Of my eyes, if I were to lose one — they are equally precious — I could doom neither; that which perished should go to its destruction without being sentenced by me. I cannot choose which of my two eyes should become blind.

"Therefore, most modest Queen, the one of my two wooers who best loves me and has the truest title in his love, let him take off my wheaten garland and marry me, or else grant that I may continue to possess the rank and condition of being a virgin so that you may allow me to continue to be in your band of followers."

The silver deer vanished under the altar, and in its place a rose bush, with one rose on it, ascended.

Emilia said, "See what Diana, our general of ebbs and flows and the tides, from the center of her holy altar with sacred act advances: one rose.

"If I correctly understand this omen, this battle shall confound and destroy both these brave Knights, and I, a virgin flower, must grow alone, unmarried and unplucked."

Some musical instruments suddenly twanged, and the rose fell from the tree.

Emilia said, "The flower has fallen, and now the rose bush descends. Oh, mistress Diana, you here discharge me from your service. I shall be gathered.

"I will be married and cease to be a virgin: I think that is your will, but I don't *know* your will. Reveal your mystery!"

She said to her attendants, "I hope that the goddess Diana is pleased; her signs were gracious."

Being given signs, even when the signs are difficult to interpret, is a gracious act by a god or goddess.

Emilia and her attendants curtsied and exited.

The doctor, jailer, and wooer talked together. The wooer was dressed like Palamon, whom he impersonated when around the jailer's daughter.

The doctor asked, "Has this advice I gave you done her any good?"

"Oh, it has helped very much," the wooer replied. "The maidens who have kept her company have half-persuaded her that I am Palamon; within this past half-hour, she came smiling to me, and asked me what I would eat, and when I would kiss her. I told her, 'Immediately,' and I kissed her twice."

"That was well done," the doctor said, "but twenty times would have been far better, for there the cure totally lies."

"Then she told me that she would stay up with me tonight, for well she knew at what hour my fit would take me," the wooer said.

A fit is a fever or a seizure.

"Let her do so," the doctor said, "and when your fit comes, fit her home, and immediately."

"Fit her home" meant "thoroughly satisfy her." In this case, it meant, "thoroughly satisfy her sexually."

"She wanted me to sing," the wooer said.

"You did, didn't you?" the doctor asked.

"No."

"That was very badly done, then," the doctor said. "You should indulge her in every way. Do whatever she wants you to do."

"Unfortunately, I have no voice, sir, to strengthen and help her that way."

"That doesn't matter," the doctor said, "as long as you make a noise. If she asks you again, do anything. Lie with her and have sex with her, if she asks you to."

"Hold on there, doctor!" the jailer said. This was his daughter they were talking about.

"Yes, he should lie with her and have sex with her at her request because it will help to cure her," the doctor said.

"But first, by your leave, they must be married before they can lie together and have sex honestly and virtuously."

"That's but a matter of excessive delicacy," the doctor said. "Don't cast your child away and lose her to madness because you are concerned about a lack of chastity. Other things, such as a cure, are more important. Cure her first in this way; then if she will be an honest wife, she has the path before her. She can get married after the cure."

"Thank you, doctor," the jailer said.

"Please bring her in, and let's see how she is," the doctor said.

"I will, and I will tell her that her Palamon is waiting for her," the jailer said. "But, doctor, I still think that you are in the wrong."

The jailer exited to get his daughter.

The doctor said, "Go, go. You fathers are fine fools. Her honesty and chastity? If we had to only give her medicine and refrain from doing other things that will cure her until we find out whether she is chaste, then we would be losing a fine opportunity to cure her!"

If the jailer's daughter were known to not be a chaste virgin, perhaps the jailer would not object to this particular cure.

"Why, do you think she is not honest and chaste, sir?" the wooer asked.

"How old is she?"

"She's eighteen."

"She may be honest and chaste," the doctor said, "but that doesn't matter. Our purpose is to cure her madness, and whether she is chaste or not doesn't matter. Whatever her father says, if you perceive her mood inclining that way that I spoke of, *videlicet*, the way of flesh — do you understand me? If she wants you to sleep with her, then sleep with her."

"*Videlicit*" is Latin for "namely" or "that is to say."

"I understand you very well, sir," the wooer said.

"Please her appetite, and do it thoroughly," the doctor said. "It will cure her, *ipso facto*. It will cure the melancholy illness that infects her."

"*Ipso facto*" is Latin for "by that very fact."

The jailer's daughter was suffering from unrequited love; if she believed that her love was requited, the doctor thought, that would cure her.

"I am of your mind, doctor," the wooer said. "I agree with you."

"You'll find that what I said is true," the doctor said.

The jailer returned with his daughter and one of her friends, whose job was to look after her.

"She is coming," the doctor said. "Please humor her."

The wooer and the doctor stood to the side.

The jailer said to his daughter, "Come, your love Palamon is waiting for you, child, and has been waiting a long time to visit you."

"I thank him for his courteous patience," the jailer's daughter said. "He's a kind gentleman, and I am much bound to him.

"Did you ever see the horse he gave me?"

"Yes," the jailer replied.

"How do you like him?"

"He's a very good-looking horse."

"Have you ever seen him dance?"

"No."

"I have, often," the jailer's daughter said. "He dances very finely, very prettily, and for a jig, come cut and long tail to him, he turns you like a top."

"Come cut and long tail" means "come what may." Horses and dogs can have either a cut (docked) tail or a long tail, and so "cut and long tail" means "all kinds of horses and dogs" or, metaphorically, "everything."

"That's fine indeed," the jailer said.

"He'll dance the morris dance at twenty miles an hour, and that will make lame the best hobbyhorse in all the parish, if I have any true judgment, and he gallops to the tune of 'Light of Love.'"

A hobbyhorse is a morris dancer whose costume includes the figure of a horse. In costume, the morris dancer looked like a rider on a horse.

The jailor's daughter asked, "What do you think of this horse?"

"Since the horse has these virtues, I think he might be able to be trained to play at tennis."

"Alas, that's nothing," the jailer's daughter said. "For this horse, that's not a challenge."

"Can he write and read, too?"

"He has very good handwriting, and he himself keeps the accounts of all his hay and provender. Any hostler who wants to cheat him must rise very early.

"You know the chestnut mare that Duke Theseus has?"

"Very well."

"She, poor beast, is horribly in love with that horse that Palamon gave me, but that horse is like his master — Palamon — he is disdainful and scornful."

"What dowry has she?"

"Some two hundred bundles of hay, and twenty measures of oats, but he'll never have her. He lisps in his neighing, and he is able to entice a miller's mare, which is supposed to be a model of sobriety. He'll be the death of the chestnut mare."

"What stuff and nonsense she utters!" the doctor said quietly.

The wooer and the doctor came forward.

"Make a curtsy," the jailer said to his daughter. "Here comes your love."

"Pretty soul, how are you?" the wooer asked.

The jailer's daughter curtsied.

The wooer said, "That's a fine maiden; there's a curtsy!"

"I am yours to command in the way of honesty," the jailer's daughter said to him. "I will do what you want me to do as long as it is chaste."

She then asked everyone, "How far is it now to the end of the world, my masters?"

Lovers will follow their loved one to the end of the world. Earlier, the jailer's mad daughter had talked about seeking Palamon throughout the wide world.

"Why, a day's journey, girl," the doctor said.

The jailer's daughter asked the wooer, "Will you go with me?"

"What shall we do there, girl?" the wooer asked.

"Why, play the game of stool-ball. What else is there to do?"

Stool-ball was a game played by young women, who would catch a ball in their lap. This fact led to sexual joking, such as a young woman being said to have caught two balls in her lap.

"I am happy to play stool-ball," the wooer said, "if we shall celebrate our wedding there."

"It is true that we will celebrate our wedding there," the jailer's daughter said, "For there, I will assure you, we shall find some blind priest for the purpose, a blind priest who will venture to marry us because here they are too scrupulous and foolish to marry us."

Palamon was a high-ranking Knight; only a blind priest would marry him to a low-ranking jailer's daughter because only a blind priest would be unaware of their difference in social rank.

The jailer's daughter continued, "Besides, my father must be hanged tomorrow, and that would be a blot in the business. It would make us unhappy."

She then asked, "Aren't you Palamon?"

"Don't you know me?" the wooer asked.

"Yes, but you don't care for me," the jailer's daughter said. "I have nothing but this poor long skirt and two coarse smocks."

A smock is a woman's undergarment.

"That doesn't matter," the wooer said. "I will have you. I will marry you."

"Will you surely?"

The wooer took her hand and said, "Yes. By this fair hand, I will."

"We'll go to bed then, after we are married," the jailer's daughter said.

"Whenever you wish," the wooer said.

He kissed her.

The jailer's daughter wiped her mouth and said, "Oh, sir, you are eager to be nibbling."

"Why do you rub my kiss off?"

"It is a sweet one, and it will perfume me finely in preparation for the wedding," the jailer's daughter replied.

She then pointed to the doctor and asked, "Isn't this your cousin Arcite?"

The doctor said, "Yes, sweetheart, and I am glad my cousin Palamon has made so fair a choice."

"Do you think he'll have me?" the jailer's daughter asked.

"Yes, without a doubt," the doctor replied.

The jailer's daughter asked her father, "Do you think so, too?"

"Yes."

"We shall have many children," the jailer's daughter said.

She then said to the doctor, whom she thought to be Arcite, "Lord, how you're grown! My Palamon, I hope, will grow too, finely, now he's at liberty. Alas, poor child, he was kept down with hard meat and ill lodging, but I'll kiss him up again."

Her words had a sexual meaning. She wanted her Palamon to grow — to have an erection. Previously, he had been kept down — he had suffered a lack of sexual excitement in prison and so had not had an erection.

A messenger arrived and said, "What are you doing here? You'll miss seeing the noblest sight that ever was seen."

"Are they on the field of battle?" the jailer asked.

"They are," the messenger said. "You have official duties there, too."

"I'll go there right away," the jailer told the messenger.

He then said to the others, "I must now leave you here."

"No, we'll go with you," the doctor replied. "I will not miss seeing the battle."

The jailer whispered to the doctor, "What do you think about my daughter?"

The doctor replied, "I promise you that within these next three or four days I'll make her mentally all right again."

The jailer and the messenger exited.

The doctor whispered to the wooer, "You must not leave her, but instead constantly look after her in this way."

"I will," the wooer said.

"Let's get her inside," the doctor said.

The wooer said to the jailer's daughter, "Come, sweet, we'll go to dinner and then we'll play at cards."

"And shall we kiss, too?"

"A hundred times."

"And twenty."

"Yes, and twenty."

"And then we'll sleep together," the jailer's daughter said.

The doctor whispered to the wooer, "Accept her offer."

The wooer said to her, "Yes, indeed, we will."

"But you shall not hurt me."

"I will not hurt you, sweet."

"If you do, love, I'll cry."

Near the place appointed for the combat were Theseus, Hippolyta, Emilia, Pirithous, and some attendants.

"I'll not go a step further," Emilia said.

"Won't you see this battle?" Pirithous asked.

"I would rather see a wren swoop like a hawk at a fly than this way of deciding who will marry me, since whoever loses the battle will die," Emilia replied. "Every blow that falls threatens a brave life; each stroke laments the place where it falls, and each stroke sounds more like a passing bell announcing a death rather than the stroke of a blade.

"I will stay here. It is enough that my hearing shall be punished with what shall happen — there is no way that I can prevent my ears from hearing the battle, but I will not sully my eyes with dread sights that I may shun."

Pirithous said to Theseus, "Sir, my good lord, your sister-in-law will go no further."

"Oh, she must," Theseus said. "She shall see deeds of honor in their reality, as they actually are — deeds of honor that sometimes are depicted well, either in art or in literature. Nature now shall create and enact the story, the credibility of which will be sealed with both eye and ear. Rather than just seeing it in a painting or hearing it in a recitation of a heroic poem, she shall both see and hear a real combat."

He said to Emilia, "You must be present. You are the victor's reward, the price and garland that will crown the argument's title. This battle will decide the question of who will win the title to you — this battle will decide who will marry you."

"Pardon me," Emilia said. "If I were present at the battle, I'd shut my eyes."

"You must be there," Theseus said. "This trial by combat is as it were in the night, and you are the only star that shines."

"I am extinct," Emilia said. "My light has gone out. There is only malice in that light that shows one combatant to the other combatant. Darkness, which always was the dam — the mother — of horror, darkness that stands accursed by many mortal millions, may even now, by casting her black mantle over both combatants, so that neither can find the other, get herself some part of a good name, and be forgiven many a murder of which she's guilty."

"You must go," Hippolyta said.

"By my faith, I will not," Emilia replied.

"Why, the Knights must kindle their valor at your eye," Theseus said. "The Knights will grow more courageous by looking at you. Know that of this war you are the treasure, and you must necessarily be present to give the pay to the winning Knight who serves you."

"Sir, pardon me," Emilia said. "The title of a kingdom may be tried outside of the Kingdom itself."

"Well, well, then; do as you please," Theseus said. "Those who remain with you may wish that any of their enemies would take their place so that they could leave you and see the combat."

"Farewell, sister," Hippolyta said. "I am likely to know who your husband will be before yourself by some small space of time. I pray that he whom the gods know to be the better man will be made your husband."

Theseus, Hippolyta, Pirithous, and the others exited.

Emilia said, "Arcite has a gentle appearance, yet his eye is like a weapon — a bow — bent, or a sharp weapon in a soft sheath. Mercy and manly courage are bedfellows in his face.

"Palamon has a most menacing appearance; his forehead is furrowed, and it seems to bury what it frowns on. Yet sometimes his forehead is not furrowed, but alters to reflect the quality of his thoughts. For a long time his eye will dwell upon the object he is thinking about.

"Melancholy becomes Palamon nobly. Arcite's mirth becomes him nobly, but Palamon's sadness is a kind of mirth. The two are mingled, as if mirth made Palamon sad and sadness made him merry. Those darker humors that are placed unattractively on others, on Palamon live in a fair dwelling."

Cornets sounded, and then trumpets sounded as if to order a charge.

Emily continued, "Listen how yonder spurs to martial spirit incite the Princes to their trial by combat! Arcite may win me, and yet Palamon may wound Arcite and spoil his figure. Oh, what amount of pity would be enough for such a chance event? If I were nearby, I might do harm to the combatants because they would glance towards my seat, and by doing so might omit a defensive movement or forfeit an offensive movement that needed to be done at that exact time."

Cornets sounded. The people watching the combat made a great cry and shouted, "Palamon!"

Emilia continued, "It is much better that I am not there. Oh, it would be better to have never been born than to be the cause of such harm!"

An attendant arrived.

"What is happening?" Emilia asked.

"They are shouting, 'Palamon!'" the attendant answered.

"Then he has won," Emilia said. "It was always likely that he would win. If you look at him, you see all grace and success, and he is without a doubt the best and first of men. I ask you to run and tell me how it goes."

People shouted and cornets sounded, and the cry of "Palamon!" filled the air.

The attendant said, "Still they cry, 'Palamon.'"

"Run and inquire about what is happening," Emilia ordered.

The attendant exited.

Emilia looked at the miniature pictures of Arcite and Palamon. Both of them were her servants in the sense they thought they were serving the woman they loved.

Addressing the picture of Arcite, she said, "Poor servant, you have lost. Upon my right side, I always wore your picture. I wore Palamon's picture on my left side — why, I don't know. I had no reason for wearing it there; I wore it there by chance. On the sinister — left — side, the heart lies; this was an omen that Palamon had the most auspicious chance of success in the battle."

Another cry and shouts went up, and cornets sounded.

Emilia said, "This burst of clamor is surely the end of the combat."

The attendant returned and said, "They said that Palamon had Arcite's body within an inch of the pillar, and so the cry was generally 'Palamon!' But soon, Arcite's assistants made a brave rescue of him, and the two bold claimants to your title and hand are at this instant hand to hand in combat."

Emilia said, "Were Arcite and Palamon to be metamorphosed into one man — why, there is no woman who is worth a composite man like that! Their single share of nobleness peculiar to each of them already causes any living, breathing lady to suffer the disadvantage of being inferior to them, of having a shortage of value in comparison to them."

Cornets sounded. The audience cried, "Arcite! Arcite!"

"More shouts?" Emilia said. "Are they still crying, 'Palamon'?"

"No," the attendant said. "Now they are crying, 'Arcite.'"

"Please pay attention to the cries," Emilia said. "Listen with both of your ears."

Cornets sounded. A great shout rose up, and the audience cried, "Arcite! Victory!"

The attendant said, "The cry is "Arcite!" and "Victory! Look, Arcite, victory!" The combat's end is proclaimed by the wind instruments."

Emilia said, "Even a half-blind person could see that Arcite was no babe. By God's eyelid, Arcite's richness and splendidness of spirit appeared from within him; it could no more be hidden in him than a fire can be hidden in flax, or than humble riverbanks can go to a court of law and sue the waters that driving winds force to rage and flood.

"I thought that good Palamon would lose the battle, yet I don't know why I thought so. Our logical reasons are not prophets although often our imaginative fancies are. They are coming off the field of battle. It's a pity! Poor Palamon!"

Cornets sounded. Theseus, Hippolyta, Pirithous, the victorious Arcite, and some attendants arrived.

Theseus said, "Look, our sister-in-law is waiting expectantly, but she is still quaking and unsettled.

"Fairest Emily, the gods by their divine verdict have given you this Knight to be your husband. He is as good a Knight as any who ever struck a blow at someone's head."

He then said to Emilia and Arcite, "Give me your hands. Arcite, you receive her, and Emilia, you receive him. Accept each other as your spouse. Become engaged to marry with a love that grows as you grow old and decay."

Arcite said, "Emily, to buy you I have lost what's dearest to me — my friend Palamon. He is dearest to me except for what I have bought, which is you. And yet I think that I have made my purchase cheaply, when I consider how highly I rate you."

"Oh, beloved sister-in-law," Theseus said, "he speaks now of Palamon, who is as brave a Knight as ever spurred a noble steed. Surely the gods want him to die a bachelor, lest his children should appear in the world as too godlike. Palamon's behavior so charmed me that I thought Hercules was an ingot of lead compared to him. But even if I would praise each part of Palamon the way I have praised the whole Palamon, your Arcite would not lose by it, for he who was that good has yet encountered his better — Arcite is better than the much-praised Palamon. I have heard two emulous Philomels — nightingales — beat the ear of the night with their contentious throats. Now one sang the higher, and then the other did, and then again the first did, one out-breasting the other until the senses could not judge between them which of the two was the better. So it fared for a good amount of time between these kinsmen, until the Heavens made one the winner by a little."

Theseus said to Arcite, "Wear with joy the garland that you have won."

He then ordered, "As for the defeated, give them our immediate justice, since I know their lives now are only a torment to them. Let the executions be done here. The scene's not for our seeing. We will go from here very joyfully, but with some sorrow."

He said to Arcite, "Take your prize by the arm. I know you will not lose her."

He then looked at his wife and said, "Hippolyta, I see one eye of yours conceives a tear, which it will deliver."

"Is this winning?" Emilia said. "Oh, all you Heavenly powers, where is your mercy? Except that your wills have said it must be so, and your wills charge me to live to comfort this unfriended, miserable Prince, who has cut away a life from him — a life more worthy than all women — I should die and I would wish to die, too."

Hippolyta said, "It is an infinite pity that four such eyes should be so fixed on one woman with the result that two eyes must necessarily be blind in death as a result of it."

"So it is," Theseus said.

A guard entered with Palamon and his three Knights; all of the prisoners were tied up. The jailer, an executioner, and others arrived. The executioner was carrying an ax. Palamon and the three Knights who had fought with him were sentenced to die by beheading. A chopping block had already been set up on a platform.

Palamon said to his Knights, "There's many a man alive who has outlived the love of the people; yes, and in the same situation stands many a father with his child. Some comfort we have by so thinking. We will die, but not without men's pity. We have men's good wishes that we should continue to live. By dying now, we avoid the loathsome misery of old age, beguile the gout and catarrh that in the last hours of life wait for gray-haired men who are approaching their graves. By dying now, we come towards the gods young and unwearied, not limping under the weight of many old sins. We surely shall please the gods better than such old sinners, and the gods will give us nectar to drink with them because we will be spirits with fewer sins than if we had lived a long time. My dear kinsmen, whose lives are laid down for this poor comfort that I have just spoken about, you have sold your lives too, too cheaply."

The First Knight said, "What death could be happier? Over us the victors have had good fortune, which is as momentary as to us death is certain. They defeated us through good luck. Their honor does not outweigh our honor by even a grain."

The Second Knight said, "Let us tell each other farewell, and with our patience let us anger unsteady Lady Fortune, who even at her steadiest reels."

Lady Fortune is often depicted in works of art as standing on a ball.

The Knights embraced each other.

"Who will be the first to die?" the Third Knight asked.

Palamon said, "He who led you to this banquet shall be the taster to you all. I will die first."

Kings employed people who would taste food to see if it was poisoned before the Kings ate it.

Palamon said to the jailer, "Ah, my friend, my friend, your gentle daughter gave me freedom once; you'll see to it just now that I am given freedom forever.

Please, tell me, how is your daughter? I heard she was not well; her kind of illness — madness — has caused me some sorrow."

"Sir, she's well restored," the jailer said, "and she will be married soon."

"By my short life, I am very glad to hear it," Palamon said. "It is the very last thing I shall be glad of. Please, tell her that. Commend me to her, and to increase the amount of her dowry, give her this."

He gave money to the jailer.

The First Knight said, "Let's all be givers and increase the amount of her dowry."

The Second Knight asked, "Is she a maiden — a virgin?"

"Truly, I think so," Palamon said. "She is a very good creature, and she deserves more from me than I can give her or speak of."

All three Knights said, "Commend us to her. Give her our compliments."

They gave money to the jailer.

The jailer accepted the money and said, "May the gods reward you all and make my daughter thankful!"

Palamon said, "*Adieu*, and let my life be now as short as my leave-taking."

He put his head on the chopping block.

The First Knight said, "Lead, courageous cousin."

The Second and Third Knights said, "We'll follow cheerfully."

A great noise sounded. People shouted, "Run! Save! Stop!"

A messenger ran quickly over to the executioner and said, "Stop, stop! Oh, stop, stop, stop!"

Pirithous arrived and ran quickly over to them and said, "Stop! It is a cursed haste you have made if you have already killed Palamon!"

Seeing Palamon, he said to him, "Noble Palamon, the gods will show their glory in a life that you are yet to lead. You won't die yet."

Palamon asked, "How can that be when I have said that Venus is false? What has happened?"

Pirithous said, "Stand up, great sir, and hear tidings that are both most dearly sweet and bitter."

Palamon stood up and asked, "What has awakened us from our dream?"

An attendant untied his hands.

"Listen," Pirithous said. "Your cousin Arcite mounted a steed that Emily first gave to him — a black one, with not a single white hair, which some will say lowers his price, for many will not buy an otherwise good horse that has this bad characteristic; this is a superstition that people here believe."

According to that superstition, an all-black horse is a vicious horse.

Pirithous continued, "Riding on this horse, Arcite trotted the stones of Athens — which the heels of the horse's shoes tapped as if it were counting rather than trampled, for the horse would make the length of his stride a mile, if it pleased his rider to put mettle in him.

"The black horse thus went counting the flinty pavement, dancing, as it were, to the music its own hooves made — for, as they say, from iron came music's origin."

According to folklore, a blacksmith whose hammers rang out different notes when striking the anvil invented music. In one folktale, the Greek philosopher Pythagoras visited a blacksmith shop and invented music.

Pirithous continued, "An envious piece of flint, cold as the old god Saturn, and like him possessed with malevolent fire, may have darted a spark when struck by a horseshoe. Or else it was fierce sulphur, aka brimstone, expressly made for the purpose of spooking Arcite's horse. I won't comment on which I think it was, but the hot horse, hot as fire, took fright and shied at it and began to do whatever misconduct its power and strength could give its will. It jumped and stood upright, having forgotten what it learned in the stable where it was trained to properly obey its rider. Like a pig, it cried in pain as Arcite used the sharp rowel of his spurs. It fretted at the use of the spurs rather than obey them even a little. It sought to use all the foul means of boisterous and rough jades' tricks to unseat Arcite, its lord who bravely kept his seat."

Jades are bad horses.

Pirithous continued, "When nothing served, when the strap under the horse's jaw would not crack, nor the strap under its belly break, nor different leaps and plunges uproot its rider from the saddle and instead Arcite kept the horse between his legs, then on its hind hoofs the horse stood up, and Arcite's legs were higher than his head. For a moment, the figures seemed to hang in the air with a strange magic. Arcite's victor's wreath then fell off his head, and immediately the jade fell over backward, and his full weight fell on Arcite and became his — the rider's — load.

"Arcite is still living, but his life is a vessel that floats only until the next wave comes and hits it. He much desires to speak with you.

"Look, here he comes."

Theseus, Hippolyta, Emilia, and Arcite appeared. Attendants carried the dying Arcite in a chair. As they approached, attendants untied the hands of the three Knights who had fought with Palamon.

Palamon said, "Oh, this is a miserable end to our friendship! The gods are mighty, Arcite. If your heart, your worthy, manly heart, is still unbroken, tell me your last words. I am Palamon, one who still loves the dying you."

Arcite said, "Emilia is yours. Take her, and with her take all the world's joy.

"Reach out your hand to me. Farewell. I have reached my last hour, and the bell that announces the end of my life is tolling.

"I was false, yet never treacherous."

He meant that he was false in not allowing Palamon to pursue Emilia without his competition because Palamon had first seen her and had first loved her. Yet his — Arcite's — love for and pursuit of Emilia had not been treacherous because he had sincerely loved Emilia.

Arcite added, "Forgive me, cousin. I want one kiss from fair Emilia."

She kissed him.

Arcite said, "It is done. Take her. I die."

He died.

Palamon said, "May your brave soul seek Elysium, the abode of honorable men in the Land of the Dead!"

Emilia said, "I'll close your eyes, Prince. May the blessed souls be with you! You are a very good man, and as long as I live, I will devote the anniversaries of this day to tears."

Palamon said, "And I will devote them to honor."

Theseus said, "In this place you two first fought; exactly here is where I separated you and stopped you from fighting. Acknowledge to the gods our thanks that you are living. Arcite's part in life has been played, and though his part was too short, he played it well. Your days of life have been lengthened, and the blissful dew of Heaven sprinkles on you.

"Powerful Venus has well graced her altar, and given you your love. Our master, Mars, has made good his oracle, and to Arcite he gave the grace — the victory — of the battle. So the deities have shown due justice."

He then ordered, "Carry Arcite's body away to be buried."

Palamon said to the body, "Oh, cousin, what a pity that we should desire things that cost us the loss of our desire. It's a pity that nothing could buy dear love except the loss of dear love."

Some attendants carried away Arcite's body.

Theseus said, "Lady Fortune never played a subtler game. The conquered Knight has the triumph, while the victorious Knight has the loss, yet in this contention the gods have been most equitable and just."

He then said, "Palamon, your kinsman Arcite confessed that the right to the lady Emilia was yours because you first saw her and at that time you proclaimed that you loved her. He restored her as if she were your stolen jewel and he requested your spirit to send him forgiven to the afterlife.

"The gods took my justice from my hand. I have the power of life and death over my subjects, but here the gods took that power for themselves.

"Lead your lady, Emilia, away, and call your friends — the three Knights who fought with you — away from the platform of death where the chopping block is located. I adopt these three Knights as my friends.

"For a day or two, let us look and be sad and pay proper attention to the funeral of Arcite.

"After the funeral, we'll put on the happy faces of bridegrooms and smile with Palamon — for whom just one hour ago I was as dearly sorry for as I was glad for Arcite, and now I am as glad for Palamon as I am sorry for Arcite."

Theseus then prayed, "Oh, you Heavenly charmers, you gods who work charms, what things you make of us! We laugh on account of what we lack, we are sorry on account of what we have, and always we are children in some way.

"Let us be thankful for that which is, and with you gods we will leave disputes that are above our heads and that we cannot resolve."

He then said to everybody present, "Let's go now and conduct ourselves in a manner appropriate to this time."

EPILOGUE

Back in William Shakespeare's day, the boy who has played Emilia in a production of the play comes out on stage and says this:

"I would now ask you how you like the play,

"But, as it is with schoolboys, cannot say [am tongue-tied].

"I am cruel [very] fearful! Pray [Please] yet stay a while,

"And let me look upon you. [Will] No man smile?

"Then it goes hard [for us], I see. He that [who] has

"Loved a young handsome wench, then, show his face —

"It is strange if none be here — and, if he will,

"Against his conscience let him hiss and kill [ruin]

"Our market [profits]. It is in vain, I see, to stay [prevent] you.

"Have at [Let's face] the worst [that] can come, then! Now what say you?

"And yet mistake me not: I am not bold [being impudent].

"We have no such cause [reason to be impudent]. If the tale we have told —

"For it is no other [nothing other than a story] — [in] any way content you
—

"For to [do] that honest purpose it was meant [for] you —

"We have our end [done what we intended to do]; and you shall have ere [before] long,

"I dare say, many a better [play], to prolong

"Your old loves [and patronage] to us. We, and all our might [all we can do],

"Rest at your service. Gentlemen, good night."

Appendix A: About the Author

It was a dark and stormy night. Suddenly a cry rang out, and on a hot summer night in 1954, Josephine, wife of Carl Bruce, gave birth to a boy — me. Unfortunately, this young married couple allowed Reuben Saturday, Josephine's brother, to name their first-born. Reuben, aka "The Joker," decided that Bruce was a nice name, so he decided to name me Bruce Bruce. I have gone by my middle name — David — ever since.

Being named Bruce David Bruce hasn't been all bad. Bank tellers remember me very quickly, so I don't often have to show an ID. It can be fun in charades, also. When I was a counselor as a teenager at Camp Echoing Hills in Warsaw, Ohio, a fellow counselor gave the signs for "sounds like" and "two words," then she pointed to a bruise on her leg twice. Bruise Bruise? Oh yeah, Bruce Bruce is the answer!

Uncle Reuben, by the way, gave me a haircut when I was in kindergarten. He cut my hair short and shaved a small bald spot on the back of my head. My mother wouldn't let me go to school until the bald spot grew out again.

Of all my brothers and sisters (six in all), I am the only transplant to Athens, Ohio. I was born in Newark, Ohio, and have lived all around Southeastern Ohio. However, I moved to Athens to go to Ohio University and have never left.

At Ohio U, I never could make up my mind whether to major in English or Philosophy, so I got a bachelor's degree with a double major in both areas, then I added a Master of Arts degree in English and a Master of Arts degree in Philosophy. Yes, I have my MAMA degree.

Currently, and for a long time to come (I eat fruits and veggies), I am spending my retirement writing books such as *Nadia Comaneci: Perfect 10*, *The Funniest People in Dance*, *Homer's* Iliad: *A Retelling in Prose*, and *William Shakespeare's* Othello: *A Retelling in Prose*.

By the way, my sister Brenda Kennedy writes romances such as *A New Beginning* and *Shattered Dreams*.

Appendix B: Some Books by David Bruce

Retellings of a Classic Work of Literature

Arden of Faversham: *A Retelling*

Ben Jonson's The Alchemist: *A Retelling*

Ben Jonson's The Arraignment, or Poetaster: *A Retelling*

Ben Jonson's Bartholomew Fair: *A Retelling*

Ben Jonson's The Case is Altered: *A Retelling*

Ben Jonson's Catiline's Conspiracy: *A Retelling*

Ben Jonson's The Devil is an Ass: *A Retelling*

Ben Jonson's Epicene: *A Retelling*

Ben Jonson's Every Man in His Humor: *A Retelling*

Ben Jonson's Every Man Out of His Humor: *A Retelling*

Ben Jonson's The Fountain of Self-Love, or Cynthia's Revels: *A Retelling*

Ben Jonson's The Magnetic Lady, or Humors Reconciled: *A Retelling*

Ben Jonson's The New Inn, or The Light Heart: *A Retelling*

Ben Jonson's Sejanus' Fall: *A Retelling*

Ben Jonson's The Staple of News: *A Retelling*

Ben Jonson's A Tale of a Tub: *A Retelling*

Ben Jonson's Volpone, or the Fox: *A Retelling*

Christopher Marlowe's Complete Plays: Retellings

Christopher Marlowe's Dido, Queen of Carthage: *A Retelling*

Christopher Marlowe's Doctor Faustus: *Retellings of the 1604 A-Text and of the 1616 B-Text*

Christopher Marlowe's Edward II: *A Retelling*

Christopher Marlowe's The Massacre at Paris: *A Retelling*

Christopher Marlowe's The Rich Jew of Malta: *A Retelling*

Christopher Marlowe's Tamburlaine, Parts 1 and 2: *Retellings*

Dante's Divine Comedy: *A Retelling in Prose*

Dante's Inferno: *A Retelling in Prose*

Dante's Purgatory: *A Retelling in Prose*

Dante's Paradise: *A Retelling in Prose*

The Famous Victories of Henry V: *A Retelling*

From the Iliad *to the* Odyssey: *A Retelling in Prose of Quintus of Smyrna's* Posthomerica

George Chapman, Ben Jonson, and John Marston's Eastward Ho! *A Retelling*

George Peele's The Arraignment of Paris: *A Retelling*

George Peele's The Battle of Alcazar: *A Retelling*

George Peele's David and Bathsheba, and the Tragedy of Absalom: *A Retelling*

George Peele's Edward I: *A Retelling*

George Peele's The Old Wives' Tale: *A Retelling*

George-a-Greene: *A Retelling*

The History of King Leir: *A Retelling*
Homer's Iliad: *A Retelling in Prose*
Homer's Odyssey: *A Retelling in Prose*
J.W. Gent.'s The Valiant Scot: *A Retelling*
Jason and the Argonauts: A Retelling in Prose of Apollonius of Rhodes' Argonautica
John Ford: Eight Plays Translated into Modern English
John Ford's The Broken Heart: *A Retelling*
John Ford's The Fancies, Chaste and Noble: *A Retelling*
John Ford's The Lady's Trial: *A Retelling*
John Ford's The Lover's Melancholy: *A Retelling*
John Ford's Love's Sacrifice: *A Retelling*
John Ford's Perkin Warbeck: *A Retelling*
John Ford's The Queen: *A Retelling*
John Ford's 'Tis Pity She's a Whore: *A Retelling*
John Lyly's Campaspe: *A Retelling*
John Lyly's Endymion, The Man in the Moon: *A Retelling*
John Lyly's Galatea: *A Retelling*
John Lyly's Love's Metamorphosis: *A Retelling*
John Lyly's Midas: *A Retelling*
John Lyly's Mother Bombie: *A Retelling*
John Lyly's Sappho and Phao: *A Retelling*
John Lyly's The Woman in the Moon: *A Retelling*
John Webster's The White Devil: *A Retelling*
King Edward III: *A Retelling*
Mankind: *A Medieval Morality Play* (A Retelling)
Margaret Cavendish's The Unnatural Tragedy: *A Retelling*
The Merry Devil of Edmonton: *A Retelling*
The Summoning of Everyman: *A Medieval Morality Play* (A Retelling)
Robert Greene's Friar Bacon and Friar Bungay: *A Retelling*
The Taming of a Shrew: *A Retelling*
Tarlton's Jests: A Retelling
Thomas Middleton's A Chaste Maid in Cheapside: *A Retelling*
Thomas Middleton's Women Beware Women: *A Retelling*
Thomas Middleton and Thomas Dekker's The Roaring Girl: *A Retelling*
Thomas Middleton and William Rowley's The Changeling: *A Retelling*
The Trojan War and Its Aftermath: Four Ancient Epic Poems
Virgil's Aeneid: *A Retelling in Prose*
William Shakespeare's 5 Late Romances: Retellings in Prose
William Shakespeare's 10 Histories: Retellings in Prose
William Shakespeare's 11 Tragedies: Retellings in Prose
William Shakespeare's 12 Comedies: Retellings in Prose
William Shakespeare's 38 Plays: Retellings in Prose

William Shakespeare's 1 Henry IV, aka Henry IV, Part 1: *A Retelling in Prose*

William Shakespeare's 2 Henry IV, aka Henry IV, Part 2: *A Retelling in Prose*

William Shakespeare's 1 Henry VI, aka Henry VI, Part 1: *A Retelling in Prose*

William Shakespeare's 2 Henry VI, aka Henry VI, Part 2: *A Retelling in Prose*

William Shakespeare's 3 Henry VI, aka Henry VI, Part 3: *A Retelling in Prose*

William Shakespeare's All's Well that Ends Well: *A Retelling in Prose*

William Shakespeare's Antony and Cleopatra: *A Retelling in Prose*

William Shakespeare's As You Like It: *A Retelling in Prose*

William Shakespeare's The Comedy of Errors: *A Retelling in Prose*

William Shakespeare's Coriolanus: *A Retelling in Prose*

William Shakespeare's Cymbeline: *A Retelling in Prose*

William Shakespeare's Hamlet: *A Retelling in Prose*

William Shakespeare's Henry V: *A Retelling in Prose*

William Shakespeare's Henry VIII: *A Retelling in Prose*

William Shakespeare's Julius Caesar: *A Retelling in Prose*

William Shakespeare's King John: *A Retelling in Prose*

William Shakespeare's King Lear: *A Retelling in Prose*

William Shakespeare's Love's Labor's Lost: *A Retelling in Prose*

William Shakespeare's Macbeth: *A Retelling in Prose*

William Shakespeare's Measure for Measure: *A Retelling in Prose*

William Shakespeare's The Merchant of Venice: *A Retelling in Prose*

William Shakespeare's The Merry Wives of Windsor: *A Retelling in Prose*

William Shakespeare's A Midsummer Night's Dream: *A Retelling in Prose*

William Shakespeare's Much Ado About Nothing: *A Retelling in Prose*

William Shakespeare's Othello: *A Retelling in Prose*

William Shakespeare's Pericles, Prince of Tyre: *A Retelling in Prose*

William Shakespeare's Richard II: *A Retelling in Prose*

William Shakespeare's Richard III: *A Retelling in Prose*

William Shakespeare's Romeo and Juliet: *A Retelling in Prose*

William Shakespeare's The Taming of the Shrew: *A Retelling in Prose*

William Shakespeare's The Tempest: *A Retelling in Prose*

William Shakespeare's Timon of Athens: *A Retelling in Prose*

William Shakespeare's Titus Andronicus: *A Retelling in Prose*

William Shakespeare's Troilus and Cressida: *A Retelling in Prose*

William Shakespeare's Twelfth Night: *A Retelling in Prose*

William Shakespeare's The Two Gentlemen of Verona: *A Retelling in Prose*

William Shakespeare's The Two Noble Kinsmen: *A Retelling in Prose*

William Shakespeare's The Winter's Tale: *A Retelling in Prose*